CHIP MITCHELL

* * *

THE CASE OF
THE ROBOT WARRIORS

Also by Fred D'Ignazio

CHIP MITCHELL:
THE CASE OF THE STOLEN COMPUTER BRAINS

WORKING ROBOTS

* * * * * * * * * * * * * * * * * * * *

CHIP MITCHELL

* * *

THE CASE OF

THE ROBOT

WARRIORS

* * * * * * * * * * * * * * * * * * * *

BY FRED D'IGNAZIO

* * * * * * * * * * * * * * * * * * * *

ILLUSTRATED BY
LARRY PEARSON

* * * * * * * * * * * * * * * * * * * *

LODESTAR BOOKS
E. P. DUTTON NEW YORK

* * * * * * * * * * * * * * * * * * * *

Text copyright © 1984 by Fred D'Ignazio

Illustrations copyright © 1984 by Larry Pearson

Library of Congress Cataloging in Publication Data

D'Ignazio, Fred.
  Chip Mitchell: The case of the Robot Warriors.

  Summary: The reader is asked to supply the answers
to eight mysteries which are solved by young computer
whiz Chip Mitchell.
  [1. Computers—Fiction. 2. Mystery and detective
stories. 3. Literary recreations] I. Pearson, Larry,
ill. II. Title.
PZ7.D5766Cg 1983 [Fic] 83-13529
ISBN 0-525-67140-4

Published in the United States by E. P. Dutton, Inc.,
2 Park Avenue, New York, N.Y. 10016
Published simultaneously in Canada by
Fitzhenry & Whiteside Limited, Toronto
Editor: Virginia Buckley   Designer: Claire Counihan
Printed in the U.S.A. W   First Edition
10 9 8 7 6 5 4 3 2 1

for Lisa

2216503

CONTENTS

The Case of

● *** T H E   C A S E   O F *** ●
● ********* T H E ********* ●
● ****** B U R P I N G ****** ●
● ***** C O M P U T E R ***** ●

Spring had arrived early, and Pine Hill, North Carolina, was bursting with new life. The sun was shining. The birds were singing. The streets were clogged with kids. Everyone was outside enjoying the beautiful weather.

But where was Chip Mitchell?

Chip was buried in his bedroom. His windows were closed and his shades were pulled down. Chilly night air clung to Chip's furniture and his menagerie of small animals. Shivering ferrets, hyraxes, rabbits, mice, and shrews huddled together in their dark, dusty cages.

All was gloom except for the corner of the room where a bright sun lamp lit up two large aquariums, Chip's latest experiment. Inside the aquariums Chip was building miniature worlds.

One aquarium was partly filled with water. Mounds of

1

sculpted sand and dirt stuck out of the water, resembling vol-
canic islands rising from the sea. Chip had covered the islands
with shrunken bonsai trees, tiny wild flowers, and rocks. Tropical fish floated and dived in the water. Salamanders and lizards
crawled around on the islands.

In the other aquarium Chip had planted clusters of ferns,
flowers, mosses, creepers, and vines to form a tropical jungle.
The inhabitants of the jungle world included snakes, bumble-
bees, caterpillars, beetles, and worms. Dragonflies swarmed
through the air. Orange lizards slithered through the jungle and
wrapped themselves around the miniature trees.

Chip was outside Jungle World looking in. He was dreaming
of buying more aquariums and creating other new worlds: Frog
World, Desert World, Ant World, and Roach World. Maybe
he could even turn some of his smaller pets loose in these
worlds, then see what would happen.

In the corner of Jungle World, something caught Chip's eye.
An odd-looking bug crawled behind the petal of a black-eyed
Susan and froze. It was an ambush bug, a cousin of the stink
bug and the assassin bug. It was hiding behind the flower petal
waiting to ambush an unsuspecting insect that was attracted to
the black-eyed Susan's bright orange-and-yellow petals.

The ambush bug reminded Chip of Dracula. Its flaring wings
spread down behind it looked like a sinister black-and-white
cape. The bug walked on its hind legs, reserving its front legs
with their sharp, knifelike edges for capturing and imprisoning
its prey.

As Chip watched, a honeybee landed on the center of the
black-eyed Susan. The bee had come hunting pollen. But before
it could move, the ambush bug snared the bee with its front
claws, then slapped its beak against the bee's body. Four tiny
tubes sprang from the beak and pierced the bee like hypodermic
needles.

The bee struggled for only an instant. Then it was dead, literally drained of its life. Fluids injected into it from the ambush bug had killed it and were turning its insides to mush. Like a feasting vampire sucking blood through a straw, the ambush bug began sucking out the bee's liquefied organs through its tubes.

After a moment, the bug removed its tubes from the dead bee. The bee's body fell from the flower like a discarded corn husk. The ambush bug concealed itself behind the flower petal again to wait for its next victim.

Chip watched the whole scene in horrified fascination. His nose was squashed so hard against the aquarium glass that he made snuffling noises as he breathed. His rapid breathing made the glass foggy. He felt like he was looking through an eerie jungle mist.

From outside Chip's bedroom window came a terrible shrill noise. Chip blinked his eyes as if returning from a dream.

He got up and stumbled through the dark room toward the window. The noise became an ear-splitting *WAH! WAH!*

Chip nudged the shade aside and looked down on the yard below. There amidst the high, wet grass was his best friend, Ruben (a.k.a. Legs) Feinberg. But Chip hardly recognized him. Legs was wearing a wide-brimmed feathered hat and the costume of a wandering minstrel from the Middle Ages.

Legs was pretending he was playing an invisible musical instrument. His fingers flicked expertly through empty air. Legs stared at the sky, his eyes closed. "WAH! WAH!" he sang. "WAH! WAH! WAH!"

Chip shook his head. The awful noises he had heard were coming from Legs' mouth. Legs was serenading Chip on his imaginary air guitar.

Chip threw open the window and stuck his head out into the bright sunlight.

3

Legs looked up and spotted his friend. He carefully propped his guitar against the side of Chip's house. He swept off his hat and bowed so low his hair brushed the grass. "Pleased to see that you have finally awakened, Your Majesty," he said. "But Your Highness better move fast if he plans to get to his royal concert on time."

Chip looked at his watch. "Oh, my gosh!" he cried. "The computer music contest! I'll be right down."

Chip closed his window, threw a wrinkled sheet on the two aquariums, and switched off the sun lamp. He slammed his bedroom door shut, bounded down the stairs, and crashed into Legs who had come in the front door.

"Hey!" Legs complained. "Watch the guitar, if you please. It's very delicate, being that it's over five hundred years old."

Five minutes later the boys were huffing and puffing, pulling Chip's computer, Hermes, and a bunch of speakers up the hill away from Chip's house.

Hermes and the other equipment rode on a vehicle called the Cart. The boys had made the Cart out of packing crates, a discarded pickle barrel, boards pulled off a moldering outhouse, and wheels from Legs' old tricycle. They loved to drag the Cart up the steepest hills in town. Then they bombed down the hills steering the Cart by yanking two pieces of dirty, frayed clothesline back and forth.

Right now the Cart was a wagon. The boys pulled it like draft horses, groaning as they slowly made their way up the hill. The Community Center, where the contest was being held, sat at the summit, all shiny and white.

Chip and Legs had just about made it to the top of the hill when a terrible thing happened: The Cart's clothesline came unfastened.

Both boys made a flying leap to try to catch the line, but both missed. The Cart whizzed back down the hill, rolling faster and

faster. At the bottom of the hill a fat, old oak tree sat right in the middle of the road. If Hermes and the Cart hit the tree they would be smashed to bits.

Chips and Legs chased the Cart down the hill. But it was no use. The Cart was too fast. "Hermes!" Chip shrieked.

Just then, around the corner near the bottom of the hill, came a troop of girls carrying large pillows, all of different colors. Chip shouted, and the girls looked up and noticed the Cart speeding toward them.

Instead of scattering, the girls gathered around a tall, dark-haired girl and began piling up pillows in the middle of the road. The girls stood behind the pillows bracing them.

The Cart crashed into the pillows with a loud *fwoop!* Then it disappeared. Pillows flew into the air. Girls scrambled everywhere, chasing pillows and digging out the Cart.

Legs and Chip arrived a few seconds later, panting and shaken. Chip stared at the crowd of girls surrounding his computer. "Is Hermes okay?" he asked. Without waiting for an answer, he pushed his way through the girls. The computer looked okay. He threw himself on Hermes and gave him a breathless bear hug. Legs collapsed on the ground beside the road.

The tall girl emerged from the pile of pillows behind Hermes. She kicked aside a big, purple pillow and marched up to Chip with a grin on her face. It was Kate Marconi.

Chip looked up. "Oh . . ." he gasped. "It's you, Kate."

"Yeah, it's me," Kate said. "Lucky for you we came by when we did. Otherwise your computer and that junkyard on wheels would have been creamed. What happened, anyway? Are you turning your computer into a soapbox racer?"

"No, no," Chip said, getting up. "We were heading for the computer music concert at the Community Center. The Cart's

6

rope broke, and it took off down the hill. I can't thank you enough. You saved Hermes."

"You owe me one," Kate said. "Now if you'll help us pick up our pillows we'll be on our way to the bug man."

"Bug man?" said Legs. He had buried himself in a pile of furry, orange couch pillows. "What bugs?" he said, his eyes peeking through the pillows.

Kate hoisted a stack of couch pillows on her head and frowned. "These pillows are from our Panthers' clubhouse in Marcy's basement," she said. "They're full of fleas from Marcy's stupid cat, Sassy. We're going to the exterminator to have them liquidated."

"We should have Sassy liquidated, too," muttered one of the girls.

"Should not!" Marcy cried and socked the girl with a pillow.

A moment later, the girls, still fighting and complaining, had gathered all the pillows and headed down the road. Kate turned toward Chip. "Here," she said, handing him a wad of dirty, crumpled paper.

"What's this?" Chip said.

"It's a Hacker's Dictionary," she said proudly. "I'm putting it together myself. Read it. You might learn something."

"I doubt it," Chips said. He stuffed the pieces of paper in his jeans pocket.

Kate waved good-bye as she left. "Good luck in the contest!" she called.

Chip and Legs looked Hermes over and decided that the computer had miraculously escaped any harm. "My guitar did okay, too," Legs said. He picked up his make-believe guitar and made a big show of dusting it off and tightening the strings.

The boys hitched the clothesline to the Cart with a couple of extra knots. They pulled the Cart back up the hill to the Community Center as fast as they could.

When they arrived at the center, they saw that the contest had just begun. It was being held in a small, crowded auditorium. The stage was a chaotic mess of orange and black wires, speakers, and computers. The first contestant's computer was halfway through a lively rendition of "Root Beer Rag." People in the audience were stomping their feet and clapping along with the beat.

Chip and Legs slipped quietly onto the back corner of the stage and set up Hermes. Chip connected Hermes' wires to a thick orange extension cord and plugged him into an outlet on the stage floor. Chip turned the computer on. Hermes' face appeared on the TV screen. He was smiling. "I'm ready," he said.

Chip, Legs, and Hermes waited impatiently for their turn. The boys were amazed at the number of computers in Pine Hill. And some of them were good musicians. One computer played a medley of raunchy songs from the Rolling Stones. Another sounded like a pipe organ in a German cathedral. Two computers flashed strobe lights and laser beams on the stage, in time with the music. There was even a robot. The robot looked like the Tin Woodsman in *The Wizard of Oz*. It tap-danced while it played "If I Only Had a Heart."

Then it was Hermes' turn.

Legs strolled out to the front of the stage in his roving troubadour costume. He had on his fake sword-fighter mustache and his pirate's eye patch. He bowed low (and nearly fell off the stage). There was a sprinkle of laughter from the audience. "Go for it, Legs!" someone shouted.

But Legs was unruffled. "Ladies and gentlemen," he said, "I wish to present Hermes the Musical Computer."

The audience applauded.

Legs continued, making things up as he went. "Hermes and I have been wandering around faraway kingdoms for years, playing music for kings and queens at beautiful palaces and castles. Now we have returned home and will give you a taste of these royal concerts. Our first piece will be a selection from Beethoven's *Emperor* Concerto. Hermes will perform the piano solo as well as play all the instruments in the orchestra."

Some of the people in the crowd yelled and whistled. They didn't believe Legs. Usually a computer the size of Hermes could manage only one instrument at a time.

"And I, Legs Feinberg, with my magic fingers, will accompany Hermes with my air guitar."

There were giggles from the audience. Chip growled at Legs and threatened him with his fist. This was not part of the script. As usual, Legs was hamming it up.

Legs ignored Chip. "And now," he said, "I give you Hermes the Musical Computer and Legs with the golden fingers."

Chip pressed Hermes' Enter button.

Legs strummed his guitar.

Hermes' face flickered on the TV screen, then disappeared. He emitted a big, juicy burp. "Burrrup!" he said. "Braak! Burr-rup!"

Chip looked at his computer, thunderstruck.

Legs looked at his guitar. "Pardon me," he said. "Let's try that again." He motioned for Chip to press Hermes' Enter button.

Fearfully, Chip pressed the button again. At first, Hermes was silent. Then he made a noise that was long, loud, and obscene.

The audience hooted with laughter. People whistled and applauded. "Sounds like your computer has a tummyache!" a girl shouted. People laughed even harder.

Legs turned toward Chip. "What's wrong with Hermes?" he whispered.

"I don't know," Chip said miserably.

The chief judge of the music contest came onto the stage. It was Miss Phipps, the math teacher from Pine Hill Middle School and head of the school's computer club. "What's wrong with your computer, boys?" she asked.

"We don't know," Chip said. "Maybe one of his circuits was hurt when he crashed into Kate's pillows this morning."

"Or maybe," said Legs, "Kate's bugs got him. Maybe some of those fleas in the Panthers' pillows got stuck in his wires. In fact, maybe Kate set the whole thing up, just to sabotage us."

"Forget it, Legs," said Chip. "Even a flea is too big to squeeze inside a microchip. That trip down the hill must have scrambled Hermes' brain."

"Speaking of Kate," Legs said, "look at that."

Chip looked at the back of the auditorium where Legs was pointing.

A safari of grocery carts stuffed with pillows was coming through the rear door of the auditorium. Each cart was pushed by a girl. Kate was at the front of the line pushing the biggest cart.

Miss Phipps went to the edge of the stage. "What are you girls doing in here?" she asked.

"Miss Phipps, we want to enter your contest." Kate pointed at the shopping carts. The girls were taking out the pillows, revealing computers, speakers, TV screens, and wires. "Do you have any spots left?"

Miss Phipps appeared puzzled. She glanced at Chip and Legs, then turned back to Kate. "As a matter of fact," she said, "a place has just opened up. The last computer was unable to perform. But your computer must be ready to go on immediately."

"Just give us five minutes!" Kate said brightly. "C'mon, Panthers," she called, "get the lead out!"

The girls pushed the carts up a ramp onto the stage. It took them only a few minutes to set up the Panther computer.

While the girls were setting up their computer, Chip spotted a girl, close by, tapping two fine, hairlike wires on her knee. The wires were connected to a maroon box with lots of dials on the top. Chip got the girl's attention and asked her what the wires were for. The girl looked startled when she saw Chip. She mumbled something about a "memory eraser," then grabbed the box and scurried to the back of the stage.

A minute later, the Panther computer was ready. And fifteen minutes after that, the audience was on their feet clapping wildly. They had just heard the contest's only singing computer. It sang half a dozen top rock songs—in the voices of the lead rock singers. And it accompanied itself with electronic music that sounded like drums, guitars, and an electric piano. The Panther computer was sure to be the contest winner!

Chip was impressed with the Panther computer, just like everyone else. But he wished that Hermes could have played, too. As well as the Panther computer played, Hermes still might have won. Now it was too late.

The judges reached their decision quickly. The vote was unanimous: The winner was the Panther computer. The judges called Kate up on the stage to accept the tall silver trophy on behalf of her club.

Chip watched Kate skip up the ramp onto the stage. She was wearing a long black cape, probably for dramatic effect. Chip turned to Legs. "She likes to ham it up, just like you," he whispered.

"Kate's a ham, all right," Legs said, sounding disgusted. "But she looks more like Dracula to me."

Chip turned to Legs, an expression of delight on his face.

11

"Dracula?" he said. "That's it! Dracula! Legs, you're a genius!" Chip punched his surprised friend on the arm and dashed up on the stage.

First he picked up one of the Panthers' pillows and buried his nose in it. He threw the pillow down. "Ah, ha!" he yelled.

He headed for Miss Phipps. Miss Phipps was lugging the heavy trophy across the stage to present it to Kate. Chip grabbed the trophy and shouted, "Hold everything! This trophy doesn't belong to the Panthers. They won the contest by cheating!"

There were gasps, shouts, and shrieks from the kids in the audience. A dozen Panthers poured onto the stage and grabbed Chip. He thrashed and kicked, but the girls held him tight. They ripped the trophy out of his hands and gave it to Kate.

"Get him out of here!" Kate said in a loud, angry whisper.

The Panthers dragged Chip down the ramp off the stage.

Kate turned to the crowd in the auditorium and said, "The Panthers thank you for this silver cup. We won the contest fair and square, and we're not giving the cup back. Chip Mitchell is just a sore loser. Anyway, all his computer can do is make gross noises."

"Let me at her!" Chip shouted and broke away from the girls. He climbed back on the stage and sprang at Kate.

"Watch it, boy!" Kate growled. "I'm an expert in kung fu. And I'd just love to break your leg." She assumed a fighting stance and waited for Chip's attack.

Miss Phipps stepped in between the two. "Stop it, stop it!" she screamed. "This has gone far enough!"

She grabbed Kate and Chip by the hand. "All right now," she said. "The Panther computer was marvelous. It deserved to win the contest. But Charles Mitchell, here, says the Panthers cheated." She looked at Chip. "Suppose you tell us all how they managed to do that," she said.

WHY SHOULDN'T THE PANTHER COMPUTER WIN THE CONTEST? WHY DOES CHIP THINK THAT THE PANTHERS CHEATED?

(For the solutions, turn to page 86.)

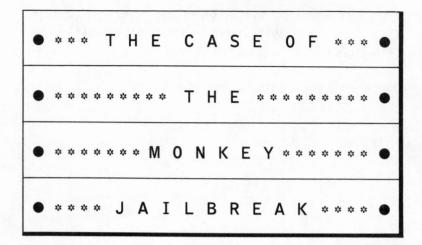

● * * * T H E   C A S E   O F * * * ●
● * * * * * * * * * T H E * * * * * * * * * ●
● * * * * * * * M O N K E Y * * * * * * * ●
● * * * * J A I L B R E A K * * * * ●

When Chip came home from school one afternoon, there was a big package waiting for him in the kitchen. Aunt Libby was dancing around the kitchen table, singing, "It's a birthday present from your father. I know what it is, but I won't tell."

Chip got a carving knife out of the kitchen drawer beside the refrigerator and went to work on the package. Plastic popcorn, straw, and crumpled newspaper flew into the air.

Chip lifted a plastic bag filled with circuit boards out of the box. He read the directions on the bag. "It's a robot!" he cried. "My very own robot!"

Aunt Libby had stopped dancing. "I knew it! I knew it!" she exclaimed. She leaned over Chip's shoulder and peered into the box. She picked up the robot's aluminum arm and its clawlike hand. "Doesn't look like a robot to me, though," she said. "I think it looks more like a giant can opener."

Chip gave his aunt a threatening look, then he continued unpacking the robot. He pried the robot's wheels, chassis, and head loose from the molded Styrofoam. Then he removed its computer circuit boards and its three batteries. One battery was for the wheels, one was for the head and arm, and one was for the robot's computer and sensors. He phoned Legs, and the two boys spent the next three afternoons and evenings on the kitchen floor putting the little robot together and learning how to program it in Robot BASIC. On the second evening, Legs went home early, but Chip stayed up until midnight writing a special program for when the robot first met Chip's pets.

When the boys were finished building and programming the robot, they went to the library and checked out books on naming a baby. The boys spent hours trying to pick out just the right name for the robot. They considered Erasmus, Horatio, Enoch, and Alexander the Great. These names had good meanings but they made the robot sound like a stuffed shirt. They thought about Oliver, Boliver, and Butt, but these were too silly.

"How about Sherwin?" Legs asked, finally, looking up from his book. "That's a simple name. And it says Sherwin means 'bright friend.'"

"Yeah," Chip said. "I like it." He threw down a book he was reading called *Name Your Cute Snookums*. "C'mon. Let's take Sherwin upstairs to meet Hermes and my other pets."

The boys grabbed the robot and carried him gently up to Chip's bedroom. One of the boys could have lifted Sherwin all by himself. The robot stood only twenty-one inches tall and weighed less than forty pounds. But to Chip and Legs, Sherwin was a pet—a fragile, expensive pet. And neither boy wanted to take the chance of dropping him.

When the boys reached Chip's bedroom, they set Sherwin

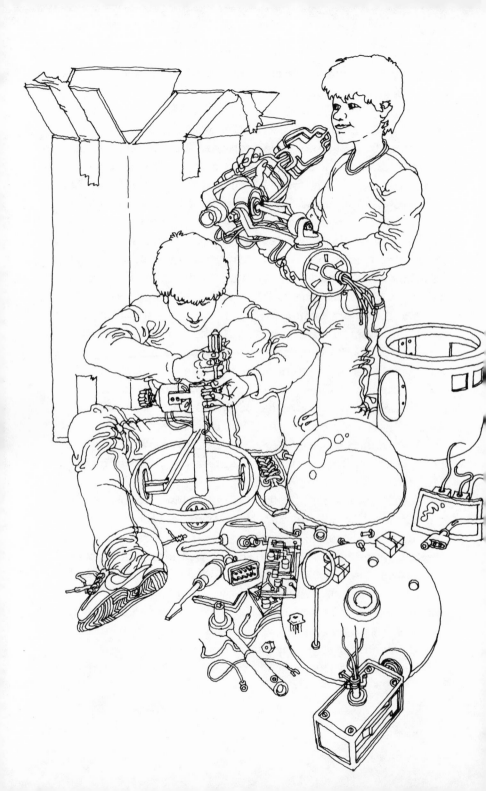

down. Chip plugged in the robot's teaching pendant, a control box attached by a cable to the robot's microchip brain. He punched in some commands in Sherwin's language—Robot BASIC.

Chip unplugged the teaching pendant. He leaned over, his mouth close to one of the robot's microphone "ears," and said "Go!"

The little robot took off. He zipped around Chip's bedroom on his shiny black baby-buggy wheels. His red, glowing eyes blinked off and on. "Wake up, creatures!" he cried. "Wake up! I am Sherwin the robot. I am Sherwin the robot. My best wishes to *everybody*!"

Chip's pets took one look at Sherwin and went crazy. Birds flapped their wings. Spring peepers hopped. Shrews shrieked, and gerbils squeaked. A tiny tree hyrax, perched on a bonsai tree branch in the corner of Chip's bedroom, let out a blood-curdling scream.

At the other end of the room was Chip's slowest animal, his rubber boa. It was probably the laziest snake in the world. But when Sherwin passed by the boa's glass tank, it thrashed about like a fire hose, then curled up into a tiny ball.

"Hey, Chip! Look up!" Legs shouted. "Look at Mandrake."

Chip looked up and saw Mandrake the monkey swinging wildly across the maze of pipes Chip had mounted beneath his high bedroom ceiling.

On the floor, Sherwin the robot had stopped moving and was now standing still. His head rotated as he scanned Chip's room.

Mandrake dropped, catlike, behind Sherwin and began sneaking up on him.

The monkey came closer and closer. All of a sudden the robot stopped rotating his head and started moving. He rolled around Mandrake in a circle. He went faster and faster. The confused monkey spun around trying to follow the robot. He got so dizzy he almost fell down.

The robot stopped and rotated his head to face the monkey. "Monkey alert! Monkey alert!" he said. "Escaped monkey! Call Chip!" Then he bellowed like a buffalo.

"Eeeeep! Eeeeep!" cried Mandrake. He scrambled up Chip's body and leaped from Chip's head to his cage, which sat atop Chip's bookshelf. He climbed inside, retreated to the rear corner, and hid under his pillow.

"Wow!" said Legs. "How did Sherwin do that?"

"Ultrasonics," Chip said, grinning. He turned down the voice volume switch on Sherwin's body.

"Ultra what?" Legs asked. He picked up a tiny, quivering deer mouse and tucked him under his sweater.

"Ultrasonics," Chip repeated. "High-pitched sound, beyond human hearing. My bats can do it, too, because they can't see worth beans. Their high-pitched squeaks act like radar. They bounce them off objects around them. When the sound comes back, it tells the bat how far away things are and what they look like."

"Sherwin squeaks like a bat?" Legs asked. He kneeled down and examined the little robot. The deer mouse crawled out of the collar of Legs' sweater and hopped onto Sherwin's head.

"Sort of," Chip answered. "But Sherwin's only programmed to recognize certain things."

"Like escaped monkeys?" Legs asked.

"Right," said Chip. "I programmed Sherwin to notice objects that don't move, like chairs and tables. That way he doesn't bump into them when he tries to go somewhere.

"And I also programmed him to ignore moving objects as tall as you or me, or a little bit smaller, like Aunt Libby. He's only supposed to watch out for very large or very small objects."

"Like trucks and monkeys," said Legs. "Does he know the difference?"

"Not yet," Chip said. "Right now he thinks everything that is not a table, chair, bed, a kid or Aunt Libby is a monkey."

"Happy birthday, dear Chip! Happy birthday to you!"

It was April 13 and Chip Mitchell's thirteenth birthday. Aunt Libby had baked Chip a giant, lopsided, angel food birthday cake. Legs had decorated the cake and it looked delicious, but also a little bit strange. On the top, for example, Legs had squirted purple cake frosting in the shape of a computer. Underneath, in green frosting, Legs had written something in computer language:

01000011 01010010 01000001 01011010 01011001

01010100 01001111 01010011 01010100 01001001 01010100 01001111 01010011

Chip hoped it said Happy Birthday. But, knowing Legs, he was pretty sure it didn't.*

Around Chip at the kitchen table sat his three best friends. Only one of them was human. They were all singing "Happy Birthday."

Chip's best *human* friend, Legs, sang in a scratchy, Motown falsetto while he strummed his air guitar.

Chip's computer, Hermes, sang in a deep but tinny voice. His voice sounded like a tobacco auctioneer singing through a sooty stovepipe.

---

*To decode Legs' message, look at Kate's computer worms on page 119. Or see "The Case of the Computer Burglar," in *Chip Mitchell: The Case of the Stolen Computer Brains,* page 40.

The third guest at Chip's birthday party was Sherwin. The robot sang in a sticky, flypaper tenor punctuated by occasional buzzes, clicks, and bleeps.

"A toast! A toast!" Legs cried. Legs and Chip raised mugs of Dr. Pepper. Hermes flashed a picture of a mug on his video screen. Sherwin raised a mug, too, in his one clawlike hand.

The mug was supposed to be empty. After all, Sherwin did not really "drink" anything. But it wasn't empty. It was full of Dr. Pepper.

But only for a moment.

When Sherwin raised the mug to toast Chip, he tipped the mug. Out poured Dr. Pepper all over Sherwin, all over the birthday cake, and all over the floor.

"Oh, no," Chip groaned.

"Don't yell at Sherwin," Legs said. "He's only three days old."

Legs ran over to the cupboard, grabbed a roll of paper towels, and ripped off two huge wads. He threw these on the floor, hopped on them, and began skating around the kitchen.

Chip wiped Sherwin off with a sponge. The little robot didn't know it had done anything wrong. Over and over it sang, "Happy birthday, dear Chip! Happy birthday to you!"

It was the day after Chip's birthday. Chip jogged home from school after track practice. He fixed a quick dinner for himself and his pets. Then, just as it was getting dark, he went to the work shed out in the backyard to help his Aunt Libby.

Before he went outside, he put all of his animals back in their cages and locked the door to his bedroom from the outside. Then he carried Sherwin downstairs and left him in the kitchen.

Aunt Libby was a sculptor. But she didn't make things out of marble or clay. She made them out of metal. Chip really liked most of the things she made. They reminded him of dinosaur heads, mermaids, and deformed ice cream cones.

When Chip's mom died, Aunt Libby kind of "adopted" Chip and treated him as her own son. Chip's dad was a computer consultant for oil companies and traveled all over the world. Since he was rarely home, he had decided to move Chip out of Pine Hill and send him away to a boarding school in Pennsylvania.

But Aunt Libby had stepped in and had invited Chip to live with her. Chip was thrilled. He could keep going to his old school and be near his old friends.

Chip often helped Aunt Libby work. This time he and his aunt worked far into the night. She was making a sculpture for the state university in Raleigh, North Carolina. And it was due at the university in less than a week.

The sculpture resembled two huge, slanted triangles rolling down a hill. Aunt Libby was welding the final pieces of one of the triangles together. She and Chip had on welding masks, welding aprons, and thick welding gloves.

Chip used a clamp to pin the two legs of the triangle together against a vise while Aunt Libby welded with her king-sized blowtorch. White, fiery sparks bounced off the metal sculpture and danced around the room. Even with the goggles on, Chip felt blinded, as though he were looking directly at the sun.

Just then, Chip and his aunt heard a bellowing noise. It sounded like a buffalo!

Aunt Libby shut off the tap on the cylinder of gas that fed the torch. After the bright light from the welding, the room seemed as dark as the cloudy, moonless night outside.

Again the bellowing sound. And this time there was a thumping noise, like a bat flying against a window. It was coming from the back of the house, from the kitchen.

21

Aunt Libby grabbed a flashlight off the top of her worktable. With Chip following her, she went to the door of the shed. She opened the door and turned on the flashlight. A beam of light stabbed through the darkness and illuminated the kitchen storm door. Aunt Libby gasped. "What's that?" she cried.

Chip looked at the door. "Cripes!" he said. "It's Sherwin!" He looked again. The little robot's head was just visible through the bottom pane of glass in the storm door. The robot was ramming himself against the glass and bellowing.

"Just your robot is it?" said Aunt Libby. "But what's that he's saying? It sounds something like 'minkey' or 'monkey.'"

"He thinks Mandrake is loose," Chip said, frowning. "He's programmed to spot Mandrake whenever he sneaks out of his cage. That's because Mandrake opens all the other animals' cages, and they have a giant party and wreck my room."

"Mandrake must have come downstairs," said Aunt Libby. "Maybe he was headed into the kitchen to raid the refrigerator." She began running toward the house. "We'd better get inside," she said. "If that monkey of yours is loose, he and your animals could wreck the whole house!"

"No, Aunt Libby!" Chip cried. He chased after his aunt. She had almost reached the back door. The only way Chip could stop her was to tackle her. They landed, hard, on top of her baby geranium plants in the garden. "Oof!" Aunt Libby said.

She rolled over. In the dark, a geranium seemed to sprout from her ear. "Why'd you do that?" she cried. "Have you gone crazy? Look what you've done to my poor geraniums."

Chip leaped up and grabbed his aunt by the arm. He pulled her up, too. "Shh," he whispered. "Don't talk." He dragged his fussing aunt back into the shed and slammed the door shut.

The shed had a telephone. Chip punched three buttons: 911. "Hello," he said. "Get me the police. There's a robbery in progress at 9514 Jones Ferry Road!"

WHY DOES CHIP THINK HIS HOUSE IS BEING ROBBED?

(For the solution, turn to page 88.)

```
● ⁂ ⁂ ⁂   T H E   C A S E   O F   ⁂ ⁂ ⁂ ●

● ⁂ ⁂ ⁂ ⁂ ⁂ ⁂ ⁂ ⁂   T H E   ⁂ ⁂ ⁂ ⁂ ⁂ ⁂ ⁂ ⁂ ●

● ⁂ ⁂ ⁂ ⁂ ⁂ ⁂   H A U N T E D   ⁂ ⁂ ⁂ ⁂ ⁂ ⁂ ●

● ⁂ ⁂ ⁂ ⁂ ⁂ ⁂ ⁂   H O T E L   ⁂ ⁂ ⁂ ⁂ ⁂ ⁂ ⁂ ●
```

"Azrael! Winifred! Puck! Come hither!"

Chip and Legs heard the deep, booming voice and froze. They had been carrying their suitcases and sleeping bags into the Marquis Hotel.

The Marquis Hotel was weird!

Chip felt as though he had fallen into a black hole in space and ended up in a hotel on another planet. The lobby was filled with *creatures*—crazy-looking people, animals, and plants.

It looked to Legs like an alien invasion. In a way it was. It was a World Science-Fiction Convention. The hotel was filled with more than four thousand science-fiction fans. And most of them were in costume.

The deep voice boomed again. The boys spun around.

Seated on the floor was a wizard. He was enormously fat. On

his shoulders was a shimmering cape that fell to the floor like the trembling slopes of an erupting volcano. His tiny head sat atop the volcano. His eyes sparkled. His Fu Manchu mustache coiled around his cheeks. He wore a hat with a picture of the ringed planet Saturn. The hat resembled a half-eaten purple head of cabbage.

Scrambling across the floor near the wizard were several of his familiars—demons, devils, sprites, and spirits that obey a wizard. They are creatures from another dimension. The wizard is their door into this world.

Familiars often take shapes of animals in this world, for example, cats, bats, and jellyfish. These familiars had taken the shape of robots.

In fact, they were robots. But they didn't look like Chip's robot, Sherwin. Instead, they looked like refugees from a video game. Their bodies were stretched out as if they were made out of bubble gum. They had long anteater noses, or no noses at all. The strangest creature had bulging eyes and elephant ears. Its body resembled a meatball. Even with its lizardlike tail, the creature was only about six inches long.

The wizard had several robot control boxes hidden beneath the folds of his cape. Chip watched him pushing buttons to control his familiars. That's like my teaching pendant for Sherwin, he thought.

"Come hither, Moloch!" the wizard called. His fingers flashed across a control box keyboard. A little octopuslike creature crawled up onto the wizard's lap. "Speak, Moloch, speak!" the wizard said. The creature snuffled as if it had a Dixie cup up its nose.

At that point, the sea of people around Chip and Legs carried them away from the wizard and over toward the elevator. The boys dived into the elevator just as the doors started to close.

A moment before the elevator door snapped shut, Chip saw

a large, handwritten sign across the room above the wizard's head. In splotchy, blood red letters, the sign read: Journey with Wyvern the Wizard to the World of K'Ardaath. See a Demonstration of the Wizard's Unearthly Powers. Come to Room 544 at Eight Tonight, *If You Dare!*

The elevator door closed. The elevator was packed with science-fiction fans. Chip needed to press the button for the fourteenth floor, but his arms were full. So he used his nose.

On the fourteenth floor, Chip and Legs popped out of the crowded elevator. They jogged to the end of the hall and entered a huge suite where their whole seventh-grade class was bunked up. Teachers were running around chasing kids and trying to stop pillow fights, water balloon battles, and toothpaste wars.

Tomorrow morning, bright and early, the class was going to Fantasy World, a new, ultramodern amusement park. Fantasy World sprawled across five hundred acres near the beach only a few miles north of Myrtle Beach, South Carolina. Its themes were science, fantasy, and the future. Chip was excited because it had some of the most thrilling rides anywhere, and the most advanced computers, robots, and electronic games.

"Beeep! Squirk! Bonk! Zap!"

Right now, Chip and Legs' hotel room sounded like a game arcade. Lots of the kids had brought handheld video games. And in the corner of the room, a crowd of kids stood around a video game on the room's TV.

Chip and Legs tossed their suitcases and sleeping bags in the corner of the room. They went to check out the video game.

The game was actually part game and part computer. The computer part was for people who stayed at the hotel on business trips. The computer was connected via the hotel intercom to the hotel's minicomputer. The minicomputer was in the room behind the manager's desk in the first-floor lobby.

You could type a letter on the little room computer and send it to the minicomputer's high-speed printer. A bellhop would bring you the letter for signature a few minutes later. Or you could turn the letter into "electronic mail." In a few seconds, the minicomputer could send your letter over telephone lines to almost any place in the world.

Or you could sit in the room and do some electronic shopping. By pushing buttons on the room computer, you could shop in the hotel's basement mall. Pictures of store products flashed on the video screen. When you saw something you liked, you just pressed the Buy button on the keyboard. A bellhop would bring the item to your room. The price of the item would automatically be added to your hotel bill.

Or the computer could turn into a calculator and let you crunch a bunch of numbers.

But Chip and Legs didn't want to mail letters or buy stuff. Instead of crunching numbers, they wanted to crunch monsters. The menu of games on the little machine was fantastic. The minicomputer downstairs piped in more than a hundred games—each for only a dime!

Up to ten kids could play a game at the same time. The kids didn't even have to be in the same room. They could be in other hotel rooms or even in the snack shop on the first floor. Chip and Legs pulled dimes out of their jeans pockets and played five other kids in a game of Griffin Grand Prix.

Griffins appeared on the TV screen along with tiny game players. A message on the screen told the young people that griffins were mythical creatures, half lion and half eagle. Chip's, Legs', and the other kids' game players climbed aboard the griffins and raced them around a track that looked like the Grand Canyon. The first player who finished a complete lap won the game.

WHIRRRRAAAOOOOW!

28

The noise started loud and got louder. It sounded like a police siren, right in the room. Chip looked at the video game. Its screen had gone blank.

"It's the hotel fire alarm!" a teacher cried.

The lights in the room blacked out.

Someone screamed. The kids around the video game all tried to move at once, but in different directions. They fell to the floor, with Chip and Legs in the middle. Chip had two kids on top of him and, for a moment, was afraid he was going to suffocate. It was like being in the grip of a thousand-legged pillow monster.

Then the beam of a flashlight tunneled through the darkened room. "Everybody calm down!" a teacher yelled. It was Mr. Janoweitz, the lead teacher for the class trip. "We've got to hurry!" Mr. Janoweitz shouted. "The elevator is probably out of order. We have fourteen flights of stairs to go down before we're out of this hotel. Everyone link hands and form a chain."

Like a giant caterpillar, the line of kids rushed from the hotel room and down the stairs. Only minutes later, they reached the heavy fire-exit door at the foot of the stairs. The kids burst out of the door into the hotel parking lot and right into an angry thunderstorm.

The teachers and the kids again linked hands and struggled around the edge of the hotel until they reached a carport at the hotel's entrance. They huddled together under the carport roof and watched hordes of wild-looking science-fiction fans flood out of the hotel's front doors.

Fire trucks roared up. Fire fighters rushed into the hotel. Chip glanced at his waterlogged digital watch. The face was steamed up. He pushed the Talk button. "Eight ten," the little watch said.

Chip looked around at the crowd. Weapons were every-

29

where. Chip saw laser blasters, medieval swords, battle axes, knives, and spears.

Many of the guests wore masks and costumes based on their favorite movie or comic book hero. A tall lady with frizzy black hair wore a long, flowing gown that had a wriggling electrical lightning bolt that flashed on and off.

Dinosaurs, dragons, and unicorns bobbed and wiggled on the shoulders of many people as they ran out of the hotel.

A hotel official appeared at the hotel's main door. He had a megaphone. "Quiet, please," he said. "I have an announcement."

A moment later, everyone was quiet. The official continued, "There is no fire. It was a false alarm."

People in the crowd all started talking at once.

"Please," said the official. "Let me explain. The hotel has recently purchased a new computer control system. Apparently there is a bug in the computer's program. The computer thought it detected a fire in a room on the fifth floor. But fire fighters have determined that there is no fire. It is safe for all of you to reenter the hotel. We apologize for this terrible inconvenience."

There were whistles and catcalls. "Stupid hotel!" someone shouted. "Stupid computer!" shouted someone else.

Chip and his classmates filed back in through the hotel's front door. The elevators were clogged with people, so they slowly climbed back up the stairs to the fourteenth floor.

An hour later, everyone was back in the hotel room having a party. Kids were drinking soda and eating all sorts of munchies. Transistor radios were blaring.

There was a knock at the door.

Legs was near the door, showing some girls a new dance step he had mastered. He danced toward the door, doing twirls and toe touches. He flew into the air trying to touch the ceiling. He

30

didn't make it, and when he landed he came down on top of the snack table. Bags of Fritos, Tostitos, and Cheese Twists exploded.

Slightly shaken from his encounter with the munchies, Legs limped to the door. A broken pretzel dangled from his left ear.

Legs opened the door. In came a hotel waiter, pushing a table on wheels. On top of the table was a huge silver bowl.

Mr. Janoweitz came out of the bathroom and collided with the table. "What's this?" he asked.

"Six dozen steamed calamari," the waiter said. "Sign here, please."

"What are calamari?" Legs asked.

"Squid!" cried Mark Panekopoulos.

Mr. Janoweitz turned to Mark. "Did you order these?" he asked.

"Nope," said Mark. "I didn't."

Mr. Janoweitz turned to the rest of the kids. "Did *anyone* order the squid?"

Nobody answered.

Mr. Janoweitz turned back to the waiter. "I'm sorry," he said. "There must be some mistake. No one here ordered this."

The waiter called the hotel kitchen. They confirmed that the order had come from the kids' room. Again Mr. Janoweitz asked if anyone ordered the squid. Again no one spoke.

Finally the waiter retreated angrily from the room, pushing his table and his six dozen calamari.

As soon as he left, a telephone call came for a girl named Joanie Donaldson. After only a moment on the phone, Joanie's face turned red. "No! Don't do that!" she cried and hung up.

"Who was that?" Mr. Janoweitz asked.

At first Joanie wouldn't answer. "The hotel desk," she said at last.

"What did they want?"

"They said a bellhop was bringing up my new purchases."

Mr. Janoweitz slapped himself on his forehead. "Oh, no," he said. "Joanie, did you use our room computer to buy something?"

"Nooo," Joanie wailed. "I really didn't."

"Well," said Mr. Janoweitz. "What was the bellhop bringing up to the room?"

"A hundred . . ." Joanie sobbed.

"A hundred what?" Mr. Janoweitz asked.

"A hundred pairs of boys' underpants."

Joanie climbed inside her sleeping bag and zipped it closed over her head.

Mr. Janoweitz ran over to the telephone and dialed the hotel desk. He asked for the hotel manager and told her about the squid and the underpants. He listened for a moment, then said, "Please fix it quickly, or we'll have to find ourselves another hotel." Then he hung up the phone.

"What did she say, Mr. Janoweitz?" Legs asked.

"She sounded very sorry and very upset," Mr. Janoweitz said. "Apparently their computer is continuing to malfunction. It's sending false orders from all the rooms in the hotel. The staff is running around trying to deliver crazy orders to all the rooms. It's costing the hotel thousands of dollars. The manager sounds like she's having a nervous breakdown. I don't know what—"

All of a sudden the lights in the room began flashing on and off. On the walls, the smoke detectors began beeping. The TV set came on. "If you suffer from a fatal case of morning mouth," said the beautiful model on the screen, "you should—"

"AWK!"

The griffin video game appeared on the screen, followed by more commercials, a female mud-wrestling match, and more video games.

The last picture to appear on the screen was a ghostly, pulsating image of the planet Saturn. Then the screen went blank, the lights went off, and the smoke detectors stopped beeping.

The room was hushed. No one dared say a word.

Then Mr. Janoweitz's flashlight came on. "I want you kids to pack up," he said.

"This hotel is haunted!" one of the kids said.

"Maybe," said Mr. Janoweitz. "But whether it's ghosts or a misguided computer, I don't care. We're getting out of here right now."

"No, wait!" Chip cried. He pushed a button on his watch. "Nine thirty," said the watch.

Mr. Janoweitz shone the light in Chip's face. "What is it, Mitchell?" he growled.

"Let me just make one phone call," Chip said. "I—I think I can maybe stop all this crazy stuff."

"Whom do you plan to call?" asked Mr. Janoweitz.

"The hotel desk," said Chip. He picked up the phone and dialed zero.

A moment later, he hung up the phone and turned to Mr. Janoweitz. "I did it!" he cried. "I've figured out who's haunting the hotel."

WHO IS HAUNTING THE MARQUIS HOTEL?

(For the solution, turn to page 89.)

```
● *** T H E   C A S E   O F *** ●

● ********* T H E ********* ●

● ****** R U N A W A Y ****** ●

● R O L L E R   C O A S T E R ●
```

"Fasten your seat belts, boys. And make sure your shoulder harnesses are good and tight."

The uniformed space shuttle officer saluted Chip and Legs, then closed their cabin door and sealed it shut.

The boys were on board one of Fantasy World's newest rides —the Space Shuttle Simulator. The simulator looked like the front part of the real space shuttle, with the back chopped off. Space shuttle simulators trained new space shuttle pilots.

"Hey!" Legs shouted, after the officer had gone. "When's this baby going to move? I'm getting— Ooop!" The simulator tilted 90 degrees backward. Legs' toes were sticking straight up in the air. "What's going on?" he gurgled.

"I think we're in launch position," Chip called out. "Hang

34

on. I have a feeling that this is the easy part. It probably gets worse from here."

The video screens on the cabin windows came to life, showing blue sky and drifting white clouds up above the boys. The simulator began rumbling. All of a sudden the boys were shoved back into their seats. It felt as if an invisible hand were pushing down on their chests. They could hardly breathe. "We're . . . taking . . . off," Chip gasped.

The pictures on the screen changed slowly at first, then faster and faster. First the boys saw clouds and sky. Then all they could see was the black emptiness of outer space. The cabin lights dimmed, and the screens filled with stars. The stars didn't twinkle, as they did back on earth. Instead, they shone like tiny flashlights, in a rainbow of colors.

The scenery was beautiful, but the next five minutes felt like five hours to spaceman Legs Feinberg. The space shuttle did things Legs didn't believe were possible. It stood on its back, on its head, and it rolled over. It even flipped completely upside down. In fact, most of the ride was upside-down.

Up above their heads, the boys could look out the cabin windows and see the earth drift by. Legs watched the earth and imagined that he was really in outer space. He prayed over and over that his seat belt and harness wouldn't snap. If they do, he thought, I'll crash through the window. He could see himself, spinning through outer space, falling back to earth like a shooting star. I'd burn up on reentry, he thought nervously. He pictured himself smashing through the ceiling of The Electric Meatball games arcade, looking like a toasted marshmallow.

The ride ended quickly. The shuttle flipped over, and the boys landed it on a superlong runway at the Kennedy Space Center, in Florida.

It took a while before Chip could convince Legs that it was

safe to leave his seat. But he finally did, and the boys climbed out of the shuttle simulator and were led to a "debriefing" room to learn more about their just completed mission.

They learned that the simulator was computer-controlled, and that all the buttons, switches, and levers they pushed were wired, via the computer, to the simulator's video screen "windows." The images in the simulator windows rotated and made the boys feel as though the simulator itself were spinning around in outer space. Actually, the simulator never left the ground and was anchored to the concrete-and-steel pavilion floor.

"I really liked the way you made the video images roll over and flip upside down," Chip said to the technician who was briefing them. "How'd you do it?"

"Ever heard of an *array*?" the woman asked.

"Sure," said Chip. "It's a way of storing information in a computer's memory. Kind of like a whole wall full of mailboxes at the post office."

"That's right," the woman said. She turned toward the keyboard at the front of the room and pressed some buttons. On the nine-foot screen above her head, a giant piece of graph paper appeared. It was snow white with green lines running up and down and from left to right. Red-, blue-, and orange-colored numbers started popping into the boxes between the lines.

"These numbers are elements in the array you see on the screen," she said. "The numbers represent the colors of each of the tiny little pixels on the video screen of the simulator," she said.

"Little pixies?" Legs asked.

"Pix*els*," the woman said, smiling. "Picture elements. They're the little points on the video screen. The computer's

36

picture is made up of millions of these little points. They're all different colors."

Chip studied the array of numbers on the screen. "I bet I know how you turn the picture around," he said.

"How?" the woman asked.

"You just pick which way you want to read the numbers in the array. For example, you could start at the top left-hand corner and just read down the rows. Or you could read across the columns. Or you could read the array upside down and backwards.

"The picture would flip around, depending on which colors the computer put in each pixel on the screen. Like this." Chip ran to the front of the room and drew a picture on the chalkboard.

"That's exactly right," the woman said, amazed. She pushed some more buttons. The earth appeared on the large screen. It disappeared, then reappeared. This time it was drawn in slow motion. It was as if a photograph of the earth were cut up with scissors into lots of strips. Then the photo was reassembled by taping the strips together, one at a time.

"When the computer does the same thing over and over, it's called a loop. We use a loop to 'spray' all the colored points onto the simulator video screens, one strip at a time," the woman said. "We can set the loop to rotate the array. And when the array rotates, the picture on the shuttle windows also rotates. It looks like you are whirling around in outer space."

"It's a neat trick," Legs said. "Was it hard to program?"

"To tell you the truth," said the woman, "it was a mess. We had all the points right, so we could draw the picture right side up. But as soon as we tried to tilt the picture or turn it upside down, we ran into problems. We ended up with pictures turning backwards and pictures being split into several pieces.

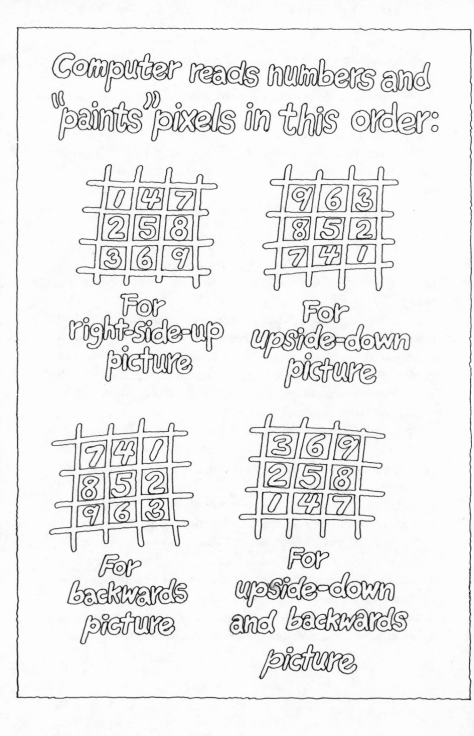

Computer reads numbers and "paints" pixels in this order:

For right-side-up picture

For upside-down picture

For backwards picture

For upside-down and backwards picture

"The key to everything was the loop through the array. If the loop didn't work, it put the wrong colors in the wrong places on the simulator screen. The pictures got all mixed up."

"How did you fix the loop?" Chip asked.

"Actually there were two loops," the woman said. "One was nested inside the other. The inside loop painted the pixels up and down on the screen. The outside loop painted them sideways. But the loops were backwards. The inside loop should have been on the outside, and the outside loop should have been inside. We had them reversed. As soon as we changed them, the pictures were perfect."

An hour later, Chip and Legs were back in seat belts, this time on another ride—the Raging Volcano. The volcano was a giant roller coaster. It was supposed to be the world's largest and the world's scariest.

The ride started about a hundred feet beneath the surface of Fantasy World. The volcano "boulder" the boys rode was a huge, disguised roller coaster car. It carried sixteen people through a clear, heavy plastic tube. Around the tube swirled colored water that resembled liquid fire.

The car blasted off, like the space shuttle leaving the earth.

According to the computer voice piped into the car, Chip and Legs were now zooming through the molten rocks at the earth's core (some 4,000 miles underground). This was where volcanoes began.

The car rushed up through the incredibly hot core and burst into the earth's mantle, an 1,800-mile-thick layer of molten "paste." Rocks in the mantle are under such incredible pressure that they have the consistency of hot Silly Putty.

The volcano car blasted through the mantle, going faster and faster. It twisted back and forth. It bounced, jerked, and turned.

Each time they changed course, Legs got woozier and woozier. His face grew pale. He had eaten a king-sized Jupiter Crunch candy bar right after he got off the space shuttle ride. Now he was worried that the candy bar might "erupt" before the volcano did.

Clouds of steam enveloped the car and lifted it up through the mantle, through the earth's crust, and into the base of an enormous volcano. The volcano was like a giant chimney in the shape of an upside-down ice cream cone. Legs and Chip's car began spiraling around the inside wall. Blasts of steam, rocks, and molten lava shook the car. Yet it continued climbing the wall higher and higher.

The car reached the narrow opening at the top of the volcano. It hesitated an instant, then plunged straight down, back into the center of the volcano.

Chip and Legs held on to the car rail. Several people in the car screamed. Around them, the volcano shrieked and roared.

"Oooh!" Legs moaned. He clutched his unhappy stomach.

The bubbling, steaming bottom of the volcano rose toward them. It looked as though they were going to crash.

At the last second, a door opened. The car rushed through the door into darkness. The volcano noises disappeared.

A moment later, the car emerged from the side of the volcano. Chip and Legs looked around as if they couldn't believe it. They were back outside! They were breathing fresh air. The sun was shining. They were safe.

The car slowed down, pulled into a station crowded with people, and stopped. The ride was over.

Chip got out of their car and pulled his friend after him. Legs weaved back and forth. His legs wiggled. He collapsed on a little tuft of grass near the station. "No more Jupiter Crunch," he said weakly. "Never ever."

After Legs recovered, he and Chip took several calmer rides, including the Antarctic Ice Trek, the Time Machine, Swallowed by a Whale, and Voyage Through a Banana Split. After a soda, the boys headed for the Fantasy World computer control room. The room was buried deep underneath the park. Chip was amazed at the number and variety of computers he saw.

Computers controlled and monitored all the park's activities, including the Raging Volcano ride. The room was filled with people sitting in front of blinking electronic maps and computer terminals. It resembled Mission Control in Houston, Texas, the command center of America's space program.

When the boys arrived, the Raging Volcano ride was just beginning again. The boys looked in awe as the volcano car with sixteen people aboard appeared simultaneously on a dozen different color video screens. To the side, a map of the car's route glowed in red and green.

"There are video cameras every foot along the car's route," the guide explained. "They monitor the car's journey from the center of the earth up to the volcano. If anything goes wrong, a siren sounds and this red light starts blinking." He pointed toward a huge red light the size of an airport control-tower beacon.

The volcano car whizzed along the pretzel-shaped track. The video cameras took close-up shots of the track, the car, and the people's faces. Nobody was smiling. Everyone was either yelling or gritting his teeth. "That's what you looked like," Legs said, punching Chip in the side.

"You looked a whole lot worse," Chip replied.

"Oh, yeah," Legs said. "Well, you—"

The big red light began flashing. A siren blared. People started shouting and running around the control room.

"Uh-oh," Chip said. He turned to the guide. "What's going on?" he asked.

"I don't know," said the guide. "This has never happened before." He stared at the video screens for a moment. Chip and Legs stared, too. The car had come into the volcano, and it was climbing the volcano's wall. It went around the edge of the wall so fast, it made Chip's head spin.

"Oh, no!" said the guide. He pointed at the large main screen in the center. "I see now," he said. "This is terrible. The car is going too fast. It's out of control."

"Isn't there some way to slow it down?" Chip asked.

"Not at this point," the guide said. He slumped into a chair behind him. "And if the car doesn't slow down," he said, "it'll fly off the track at the top of the volcano. It might even be going fast enough to shoot right out of the volcano. It's a hundred-foot sheer drop to the ground. All the people will be killed!"

Chip and Legs watched in horror as the car circled around the wall of the volcano. It would be at the top in just a few more moments.

As Chip watched the video screens he heard people shouting orders and questions. At a computer terminal close by, he overheard two men talking in loud voices. One man was accusing the other. "This is all your fault," he said. "There's a bug in your program."

"I know, I know," the other man said. His body was bent over the table. His hands covered his face. "I'm so sorry. I know the bug is somewhere."

"Where?" the first man shouted. "There's still time!"

"I don't know where," the man said. "The computer is feeding numbers to control the speed of the car motor. But it's feeding them in backwards or upside down."

Chip shuddered. The man's remark reminded him of something. Then he had it! He ran over to the two men. "I think I know what's wrong with the program," he told them. "If we fix it quick, maybe we can save the people in the volcano car."

WHAT IS WRONG WITH THE PROGRAM? HOW CAN THE MEN FIX IT?

(For the solutions, turn to page 92.)

```
┌─────────────────────────────────────────────┐
│  ●  * * *  T H E   C A S E   O F  * * *  ●   │
├─────────────────────────────────────────────┤
│  ●  * * * * * * * *  T H E  * * * * * * * *  ●│
├─────────────────────────────────────────────┤
│  ●  * * * * * * *  R O B O T  * * * * * * *  ●│
├─────────────────────────────────────────────┤
│  ●  * * * * *  W A R R I O R S  * * * * *  ●  │
└─────────────────────────────────────────────┘
```

"Hey, Karhonda!" said Sleepy. "What's happening?"

Sleepy Kolwezi, one of Chip's best friends, was wandering around Fantasy World and had just spotted a classmate. She was coming out a door of a bright yellow aluminum shed.

Sleepy ran to the shed. "What's in there?" he asked.

Karhonda looked startled. "Oh, Sleepy!" she said. "Uh . . . hi!"

Sleepy looked in the shed. It was gloomy inside. Standing in the corner were two large clothes dummies. It was too dark to see their features or what they were wearing. But they looked really big, and sort of fat. "What are those?" Sleepy asked.

"What?" Karhonda said. She looked in the shed. "Oh, them. I think they're some kind of robots."

"Robots? Let's take a look at them."

"I already did," said Karhonda. "They're boring. Just fat women in old-fashioned dresses."

"Where do they come from?" Sleepy asked. He started to shut the door. Sleepy was interested in robots, but not in fat women robots.

"I think they belong in the Time Machine Pavilion," Karhonda said. "They're supposed to be wives of some big-time king, or something. C'mon, this is boring. Let's go someplace more exciting."

"Go? Go where?" Sleepy asked. He was surprised. Karhonda was one of the lieutenants in Kate Marconi's gang. She wasn't usually this friendly.

Karhonda slammed the shed door shut and grabbed Sleepy by the arm. "You'll see," she said.

"Hey, wait!" Sleepy said. He tried to pull away, but Karhonda held on. "I was headed to see the Robot Warriors arena," he said. "They say there are real robots there, and you can control them and make them fight each other."

"Yeah, sure," Karhonda said. "We'll go there in a minute." She dragged Sleepy toward the Outer-Space Pavilion at the opposite end of the concourse. The pavilion was a geodesic dome—a giant golf ball constructed out of triangular metal struts that glittered like facets of a diamond.

"Where are we headed?" Sleepy asked.

"To the space shuttle ride," Karhonda said. "Are you coming with me or not?"

"I guess," Sleepy said. "But only if you don't ditch me on the moon or somewhere. And let go of my arm. I can walk, you know."

Not far away, Chip Mitchell and Kate Marconi were sitting on the ground in the front of a long line of people. A large display screen above their heads read, FIGHTING ROBOT WARRIORS. Chip and Kate were at the Robot

46

Warriors arena. They had been in the Robot Warriors line since before daylight. Coming here had been Kate's idea. She wanted them to be the first people to operate the warriors.

The night before, everyone had been sitting around, munching on pepperoni pizza in their huge suite at the Marquis Hotel. All of a sudden, Kate had come up to Chip and challenged him to a duel with the robot warriors.

Everyone was listening. Chip had no choice. He had to accept.

After thinking about it awhile, Chip started looking forward to the duel. He figured he could whip Kate because he had had plenty of practice controlling his own robot, Sherwin.

Besides, the robot warriors were famous! Chip had read about them even before his class came to Fantasy World. An article in a national science magazine had said that the robots were controlled by two dozen microchips. The little microchip brains turned the robots into first-class fighting machines. They could walk and talk. They could duck, weave, and dodge. And they knew how to use spears, shields, poles, and swords.

"They're supposed to be expert swordsmen," Chip, upside-down, said to Kate. He was practicing standing on his head.

"Swords*women,*" Kate corrected.

"Well—" Chip said. Then he forgot what he was going to say. Standing on his head made his eyeballs feel kind of squishy. Maybe his brain, too.

"Where's Legs?" Kate asked.

"He's entered the Jet-Powered Roller Skating Contest over at the Velodrome," said Chip. "I'm going there later to watch him."

"Hey, Chip," Kate said, "did you ever look at the Hacker's Dictionary that I gave you the day of the computer music contest?"

"I sure did," Chip said. Still upside-down, he pulled several

47

pieces of crumpled-up paper out of his jeans pocket. "Here," he said. "I added a few words of my own. I typed the whole dictionary on Hermes. Here's a copy for you."

Kate looked at the paper. "You even threw in my computer worms!" she exclaimed. (Turn to pages 111–118 and you can see Kate and Chip's Official Hacker's Dictionary.)

"Look!" said Kate. Upside-down, Chip looked.

A dumpy little man was climbing the steps of the Robot Warriors arena. Right behind him were two robots—*women* robots. The women were enormous. And they looked tough. On their heads the women wore round hats that resembled bent Frisbees. At the center of the hats were spear tips pointing skyward. Their dresses ballooned open at the bottom and seemed to be made out of chicken wire. The women wore shiny black boots that gleamed in the morning sunlight.

Chip did a quick somersault, fell down, then stood up. "They're bigger than I thought," he said.

Kate nodded her head. "A lot bigger," she agreed.

The man and the robots wound their way down the spiral steps into the circular pit where the robots would do battle. The robots and the man ducked under the rope at the edge of the ring and climbed inside. In the center of the ring was a large wooden case shaped like a casket. The man opened the lid of the case. He reached inside and pulled out two huge swords and two shields. They looked like they were made of polished silver and reflected the sunlight like mirrors.

The man fastened the weapons to the robots' arms and hands. Then he dragged the case to the edge of the ring. He climbed under the rope and pulled the case behind him.

He turned toward Chip, Kate, and the other people waiting in line. He waved his arm. "Come on down!" he shouted.

When the line of people had wound its way down into the pit, the man pointed to Kate and Chip. "You two kids—climb into the ring."

Kate and Chip slipped under the rope and stood up. Then the man had them climb up onto walled wooden platforms that resembled church pulpits. The platforms were on the edge of the ring, directly opposite each other.

"You control the robots from up there during the fight," said the man. "The robots are strong, and they're rough. You have to stay out of the way, or you'll get hurt."

The man turned toward Kate. "Girlie," he said, "you get Ra—"

Kate interrupted him. She pointed to the robot with the deadly looking machete. "I want that one," she said.

"That's Bertha," said the man. "She's all yours if you want her."

He turned toward Chip. "Your girlfriend made a bad choice," he said. "Bertha loses most battles. But you, kid, you get Rachet. Rachet's the champ. Just treat her right, and she'll win the match."

The man handed Kate and Chip metal boxes that resembled the teaching pendant Chip used to program his robot, Sherwin. The boxes send commands to the robots via radio waves.

The man taught the kids how to use the boxes to control the robots and make them fight. "Remember," he said, "the robots have tiny computers inside. They are not dumb machines. They respond to your commands, but they also have a FIGHT program running through their computers. Plus they have several sensors that send them messages from the outside world."

"What kind of sensors?" Chip asked.

"Infrared, ultrasonics, video cameras, tactile sensors, voice recognition, the whole works," said the man. "I know because I designed and built them."

49

He explained the rules of combat.

"Any questions?" he asked.

"Just one," Chip said. "Are the robots' swords real?"

"Nope," said the man. "They're made out of Styrofoam. A thin coating of metal foil on the surface makes them look real."

The man climbed out of the ring. "When I count to three," he said, "you press the red Fight button in the upper right-hand corner of the box. One . . . two . . . three!"

Kate and Chip pressed the red buttons.

The robots came to life. Rachet began grunting. Bertha let out a war cry that sent a chill through Chip's body.

Then the robots attacked.

Bertha raised her sword and sent it crashing down on Rachet's head. Electronic sensors on Rachet's body recorded the hit. She beeped loudly. On the scoreboard above the ring, the hit was recorded. Kate's and Chip's names were on the board in big, red LED letters. Under Kate's name was 100 for the direct hit. Under Chip's name was a 0.

Chip planned to change that real fast. He pressed a button and Rachet counterattacked. She swung her glittering sword in the direction of Bertha's belly button.

But Kate was ready. She pulled a switch, and Bertha raised her shield. Rachet's sword bounced off the shield and flew out of her hand. Now the score read 150 for Kate. Chip's score was still 0.

Kate seemed to have already mastered the robot controls. Yet Chip was still struggling. Finally, he got Rachet to walk to the fallen sword and bend over to pick it up. But Bertha was just behind her. When Rachet bent over, Bertha swung her sword and walloped her on the bottom.

Rachet let out a shrill electronic whine. Red lights on her bottom flashed on and off.

50

On the scoreboard, Kate now had 250. Chip didn't have to look at his score. He knew it was still a big, fat zero.

Bertha kept smacking Rachet on the bottom. Rachet got up and began running away. Bertha chased after her, swinging her machete sword up and down like a woodcutter's axe. The sword was so big, each time it came down it hit Rachet's head and made a loud *thwack!*

Round and round the ring the two robots raced. *Thwack!* went Bertha's sword. *Thwack! Thwack! Thwack!*

The audience loved watching the robots chase each other. They laughed, whistled, and cheered. Out of the corner of his eye, Chip noticed that his friend Sleepy was in the crowd. Sleepy was laughing, too.

Each time Bertha smacked Rachet, Kate scored more points. The scoreboard was a blur. Kate was racking up points like crazy: 1000, 2000, 3000. If she got 5000, the game would be over. Kate and her robot would be the winners.

Chip was desperate. He searched for a new button on his control box. He pressed a button called Rotate.

Rachet kept running, but from the waist up, her body began to spin. She spun faster and faster, swinging her sword like a buzz saw.

Chip pressed a button marked Growl. Rachet began growling. She turned and attacked Bertha.

Bertha started backing away.

Rachet came closer and closer. Then, all of a sudden, she made a right turn and headed straight toward Chip.

Chip searched for the Stop button on his control box. But it was too late. Rachet began running. And before Chip could stop her, she ran right into his platform, then bounced onto the floor of the ring.

When Rachet's metal body crashed into the platform, it felt

to Chip like an earthquake. He dropped his control box, and it fell to the platform floor.

As Chip reached for it, he looked down at the robot. Rachet got up slowly. She was acting strange. Chip pressed buttons to make her attack Bertha. But she didn't obey. Instead, she threw down her weapons and hugged the platform. Then she began pushing it.

"Back, Rachet!" Chip yelled. "Back! Back!" He madly pressed the buttons on the control box. Nothing happened. The big robot kept pushing the platform. As she pushed, she grunted.

The platform began to rock violently. Chip grabbed the top of the platform wall to keep from falling off.

The robot was uprooting the platform from its base. In another moment, Chip and the platform would topple off the ring and fall ten feet to the floor of the pit.

The robot's trainer ran across the ring. He climbed up Rachet's back to reach her On-Off switch. But Rachet was moving too swiftly. Her elbow came up, caught him on the chin, and knocked him on his bottom. He rolled across the ring and under the rope.

The audience began to scream. People underneath Chip's platform crowded into the aisles, trying to flee from the arena.

All of a sudden, Bertha flashed across the ring. She had dropped her weapons and was headed for Rachet.

"HEYYY YAH!" Bertha yelled. She gave Rachet a chop in the side of the neck. Then she raised her foot high in the air and slammed it into Rachet's shoulder.

Chip couldn't believe it. Bertha was using kung fu! Kate was an expert at kung fu. Now her robot was, too!

Bertha kicked Rachet's feet out from under her. Rachet lost her balance and toppled onto the floor of the ring. The moment she hit the floor, her trainer crawled into the ring. He raced up to Rachet and switched off her main power supply.

Rachet slumped to the floor and lay still.

Chip climbed down from the platform carefully. Sleepy Kolwezi rushed up from the audience and got into the ring next to Chip. "That was a great act," he said. "But it was close, man. Too close. Are you okay?"

"Yeah, I think so," Chip said shakily. "It wasn't an act. The robot really went crazy. And it was my fault."

He and Sleepy walked over to the robots' trainer. The trainer was examining the circuits and switches inside Rachet's dress.

"I'm really sorry," Chip said, leaning over the unconscious robot. "When I dropped the control box, it must have screwed up Rachet's signals."

"Nah, that's not it," the man said. "See this switch here?" He pointed to a small white switch near Rachet's armpit. "This is the switch that turns on her infrared detector. When that's on, Rachet turns into a bloodhound. Only she senses heat instead of smells."

"Oh, yeah," Chip said. "I remember that from an article I read. The robots can sense heat the same way as rattlesnakes stalking their prey."

"Right," said the man. "Using infrared, Rachet can sense a heated object up to fifteen feet away."

"Like my body?" Chip asked, kneeling next to the man.

"Yes," he said. "When Bertha was chasing Rachet around the ring, Rachet's infrared sensor accidentally came on. I don't know how. It has a safety lock to prevent this sort of thing. Anyway, in Fight mode, she's programmed to pursue a heated object and try to catch it."

"Why?" Chip asked.

"Both these robots were originally designed for purposes other than fighting," the man explained. "Hunters use them to help locate wild animals in the forest. The animals might be hidden and remain absolutely still, but the robots can detect the animals' body heat.

"Also, the Red Cross, ski patrols, and public safety officials use them to find lost people. The people might not be able to make a sound. They might be sick, injured, or unconscious. They might even be under a snowdrift. But the robots can find them by sensing their body heat."

Kate climbed down from her platform. Karhonda climbed into the ring and ran over to her. The two girls walked across the ring to see the fallen robot.

Chip looked up from where he was kneeling. "Kate," he said, "that was some fancy fighting you did with your robot. Thanks a lot. If not for you and Bertha, I could be in an ambulance on the way to a hospital right now."

"No sweat," Kate said, shrugging. "I'm just sorry that your robot went bonkers. I was whipping her tail off." Kate winked at Karhonda.

"Excuse me," said the robots' trainer. "But I'd appreciate it if you kids would help me carry Rachet back to the shed for an overhaul. Even with everyone helping, we'll have to make at least a couple of trips since she's so heavy."

Chip looked at the robot. The man had taken her apart.

Chip and his friends picked up the pieces of Rachet. Chip and Sleepy grabbed her head. Kate and Karhonda grabbed an arm. The man carried the teaching pendant and a circuit board he had unplugged from inside her stomach.

Everybody climbed out of the ring and walked slowly up the spiral stairs. Bertha the robot followed them, carrying a leg.

A few minutes later, the group was at the top of the empty coliseum. After Kate's robot had made its dramatic rescue, several ushers had appeared and had helped the audience make a quick exit.

Chip looked out at the other Fantasy World pavilions. "Which way to the shed?" he asked.

The man pointed toward a bright yellow shed about a hundred yards away. "Right over there," he said.

"Uh-oh!" said Sleepy. He turned to Chip. "Something has been bothering me ever since I got here. But I didn't know what. Now I know."

"What are you talking about?" Chip asked.

"I'm saying that I think I know why your robot went crazy."

WHY DID CHIP'S ROBOT GO CRAZY?

(For the solution, turn to page 95.)

```
● ∗ ∗ ∗    T H E    C A S E    O F    ∗ ∗ ∗  ●

● ∗ ∗ ∗ ∗ ∗ ∗ ∗ ∗    T H E    ∗ ∗ ∗ ∗ ∗ ∗ ∗ ∗  ●

● ∗ ∗ ∗ ∗ ∗    C O M P U T E R    ∗ ∗ ∗ ∗ ∗  ●

● ∗ ∗ ∗ ∗    S C A P E G O A T    ∗ ∗ ∗ ∗  ●
```

One afternoon after returning from their class trip, Chip and
Legs were jogging across a new cross-country trail, deep in a
forest north of their school.

"Hey! Look at that!" Legs said. He stopped running and
pointed.

Over across a small clearing was a log cabin. The door was
open.

Legs started running toward the cabin. "Let's investigate,"
he said. "It looks abandoned."

Chip followed his friend. The boys ran right up onto the
cabin porch. They stopped for a moment and peered inside the
cabin door. Inside it was gloomy and musty.

"Look at this," Chip said. He bent down and picked up a
crumpled piece of paper. He straightened it out. "It's from the

county department of social services," he said. "It says somebody named Radley Moser got a Social Security check for $165."

"Does it say anything else?" Legs asked. He was still trying to see inside the cabin.

"Nothing," Chip said. "Just Radley's number—MKW 30449. Do you think this guy still lives here? If he does—"

"Nah," said Legs. "But maybe his $165 is here somewhere. That would buy a lot of tokens at the Meatball, wouldn't it?"

Legs crept cautiously through the doorway into the cabin. Chip followed him.

"Chip!" he cried. "There's a dead body in here!" He pointed to the bed.

Chip was ready to dash out the door when the dead body spoke. "Awk," it said. "Awk!"

Legs flew past Chip, on his way out of the cabin. Chip grabbed him by the arm. "Wait!" he said. "Whatever it is, it's alive. Didn't you hear it?"

"Leggo!" Legs said, trying to escape. "I heard it! That's why I'm getting out of here!"

"Then go on," Chip said, releasing his friend. Legs disappeared out the door.

Chip walked carefully over to the dead body that was maybe alive. He heard some low groaning. "Water," the body whispered. "Water."

Chip looked around the cabin. He ran to the counter and found a half-full bucket of rusty well water. He poured some water into an empty peanut butter jar and carried it over to the bed. He knelt down.

The body in the bed was a man. It was an old man, a *very* old man. Chip lifted the man's head and helped him sip some of the water. "Thanks," the man whispered. Even when he whispered, his voice sounded crackly, like dry leaves.

Chip leaned over the man. "Who are you?" he asked.

"Radley," the man whispered. "Radley Moser."

"Oh," Chip said. He remembered the piece of paper he had found on the front porch. He had stuck the paper inside his jogging pants. He pulled out the paper and put it on a table beside the bed.

"Need food," whispered Radley. "Very hungry."

Chip looked at the man's frail, bony body. He looked half-starved.

Chip patted the man's hand. "Wait here," he said. As he said it, he realized it must sound dumb. The man wasn't going anywhere. He could barely lift his head.

"I'll bring you some food," Chip said. He stood up. Then he backed out of the room and ran out the door.

On the other side of the clearing, Chip found Legs hiding behind a rock.

"A lot of help you were," Chip said. He told Legs about meeting Radley and getting him some water. "C'mon," he said. "Track practice is over. We've got to get Radley some food."

The boys ran back to Legs' house. They found two of Mrs. Feinberg's pillowcases hanging on the clothesline in the backyard. They filled them with food from the refrigerator, and called Legs' family doctor and told him about Radley. The doctor was in the middle of an emergency, but he said he'd come over as quickly as he could. Then the boys swung the pillowcases over their shoulders and ran off toward Radley Moser's cabin.

When Chip and Legs arrived at the cabin, they mixed up some cereal and opened a can of applesauce. Radley was so weak they had to feed him like a baby. After they fed him, they sat on the floor next to his bed listening to his heavy, crackly breathing.

Gradually Radley regained some of his strength. Finally,

with the boys' help he sat up. The boys brought over a padded chair. They helped Radley move to the chair and sit down.

A moment later, Radley began to talk. In a husky, wheezing voice he told the boys how he'd come to be lying in his own cabin starving to death. "It's all the fault of that cussed machine!" he rasped.

"What machine?" Legs asked.

"The kumpewer," Radley said. He reached over on the table and grabbed an old, moldy stick of chewing tobacco. He bit off a hunk and tucked it into his cheek. A moment later, he spat into the woodpile behind his chair.

"Kumpewer?" Legs said, puzzled.

"The computer?" Chip asked.

"Yah," said Radley, chewing. "The kumpewer."

Radley explained how he had been living fine and dandy in his cabin, year after year. Every month, like clockwork, he got his Social Security check for $165 from social services. Then one month the check didn't come. Radley had gone to the social services office, and they told him that there was some problem with the computer. They claimed the computer had "swallowed" his check. They told him to come back the following month.

Radley had waited a whole month for his new check. Again it didn't come. And again he was told that it didn't come because of the computer. "Crazy, gawdawful kumpewer!" Radley snorted. "It's starving an old man to death and it don't care a durn toot!" Radley spat into the woodpile.

Legs was angry. He looked at his watch. He stood up and ran toward the door. "C'mon, Chip!" he said. "It's a quarter to five. If we hurry, we can get to the social services office before it closes."

Chip started to head out the door. Behind him, Radley called weakly, "Hold it, young fellow."

61

Chip stopped and spun around.

"Take that paper with you," Radley whispered. "It says the money is due me. And when you get there, look fer Mr. Wren. He's been helpin' me."

Chip grabbed the social services form and ran out the door after Legs.

Fifteen minutes and four seconds later the boys arrived, gasping and panting, at the Social Security payments office of the county social services department. A big man with an ID badge that said Wren 30449 was in the office. But he was carrying a briefcase and heading out the door.

"I'm sorry," the man said. "The office is closed. Come back tomorrow."

Chip and Legs tried to explain to the man about Radley Moser. But the man wouldn't hear it. He said that Moser was right: that the computer had swallowed his records. The man said the department of social services was investigating the situation. In another few weeks they'd probably have an answer.

"In another few weeks, Radley Moser will be dead!" Legs cried.

"I'm awfully sorry about that," said the man. "But it's not my problem. Now if you'll please excuse me—"

"What's going on in here?" came a voice. A man walked in the door. "Is there some problem, Myron?" the man asked.

"No, Mr. Randolph," said the man. "These kids were on their way out. I was just explaining to them that they had made a mistake. They came to the wrong office." The man began pushing Legs and Chip toward the door.

Chip was about to give up. Then he looked across the room at the lone desk. On top of the desk was a brass nameplate. It said Myron K. Wren.

Chip grabbed on to the door handle. "I'm not leaving!" he

said. He looked toward the man who had just come into the room. "Mr. Randolph," he said, "somebody here has turned your computer into a scapegoat."

"A scapegoat?" said Mr. Randolph.

"Yes, sir," said Chip. "They're cheating Mr. Radley Moser, an old man living on Social Security. And they're blaming it on your computer."

WHO IS CHEATING RADLEY MOSER? AND HOW?

(For the solutions, turn to page 99.)

```
●  ✽ ✽ ✽   T H E   C A S E   O F   ✽ ✽ ✽  ●

●  ✽ ✽ ✽ ✽ ✽ ✽ ✽ ✽ ✽   T H E   ✽ ✽ ✽ ✽ ✽ ✽ ✽ ✽ ✽  ●

●  ✽ ✽ ✽ ✽ ✽   M I D N I G H T   ✽ ✽ ✽ ✽ ✽  ●

●  ✽ ✽ ✽   C R A N K   C A L L S   ✽ ✽ ✽  ●
```

It was a week after Chip had solved The Case of the Computer Scapegoat. Chip's dad was back home again, after a lengthy business trip. It was late at night, and Mr. Mitchell and Aunt Libby were downstairs, sound asleep in their beds.

Chip was upstairs in his bedroom. He and his pets were feasting on a snack of assorted goodies inside a "bed cave" that Chip had built out of a small sawhorse and blankets. Chip was busy trying to squeeze a sticky object the size of a tennis ball into his mouth. The object was one of Chip's food inventions. It was made out of a melted Chocolate Rocket candy bar, raisins, popcorn, and maple syrup. It was held together by a rubber band salvaged from the evening newspaper.

Brrrinngg!

Chip's animals had been softly munching, crunching, and

chittering. The phone surprised them, and they started squeaking and crying.

Chip heard his aunt's voice downstairs as she answered the phone. Then she shrieked. Chip heard his father's voice, loud and angry.

What was going on? Chip tried to climb quickly out of the cave. But his foot caught on one of the blankets, and he tripped. He fell into the front leg of the sawhorse. The leg slipped over the edge of the bed. The sawhorse flipped upside down and fell on the floor. With it went Chip, his animals, the food, and the entire cave.

Chip lay on the floor underneath the blankets and the upended sawhorse. He was covered with syrupy goo from everyone's snacks. Frightened animals stampeded over his face, trying to escape from the collapsed cave.

At last, Chip managed to struggle free. He stood up and ran out of his bedroom. He kicked the door shut with his foot.

When he got downstairs, he found his dad and his aunt in his aunt's bedroom sitting on the corner of the bed. "What happened?" he cried.

His dad looked up. "What happened to you?" he asked. "It looks like you poured a box of cereal on your head."

Chip brushed cereal flakes out of his blond hair. He stuck his finger in his ear and scooped out a glob of maple syrup. "Nothing," he said.

"Well, nothing is what's going on down here, too," his father said. He had his hand on Aunt Libby's shoulder. "Just a stupid phone call. Nothing more."

"What kind of phone call?" Chip asked. He looked at his aunt. She was shaking.

His aunt stood up. She kicked a pillow across the room, into the closet. "A crank call," she muttered. "Some dumb kid playing a prank."

Chip's father turned to him. "Why do kids your age think it's so funny to call people in the middle of the night and say such awful things?" he asked. "Why?"

"What did they say?" Chip asked. He went into the closet and got Aunt Libby's pillow. He put it on her bed and hopped on top.

"The usual," Aunt Libby said. "Crank calls are all the same. They asked me out on a date. They told me they had been watching me. They said I was 'cute.' Then they told a dirty joke."

"Which one?" Chip asked. He reached in his pocket and found some soggy popcorn and a half-drowned cave cricket.

"Chip!" his father said.

"Uh-oh," Chip said. He slid off the pillow and began leaving the room. "Think I'll be going back to bed."

The next day at school, Chip was dragging. The crank call had come at midnight. Chip had stayed awake an extra hour and a half, cleaning up the mess from his cave. And it had taken him another hour to track down his escaped pets and return them to their cages.

The following morning, a hamster and a cave salamander named Big Foot were still on the loose. Something kept stepping on Chip's nose during the night and waking him up. He suspected it was Big Foot.

After school, Chip had track practice. Practice was a total loss. Chip almost threw up twice. The first time was after he ran his practice laps too fast. Then he almost threw up again when he returned to the foul-smelling locker room. The odor from the month-old, rotting socks in his own locker sent him running to the bathroom gagging.

On his way home from track practice, Chip stopped at The Electric Meatball, an electronic games arcade in downtown

Pine Hill. He needed to play a couple of games to pick up his mood. But he found the door locked. A sign on the door said that the games arcade was closed due to an order from the Pine Hill Town Council. There had been several complaints about the Meatball being a hangout and a connection for local drug dealers. That night a meeting was being held at the municipal building to determine if the Meatball should be closed up permanently.

Chip ran across the street to The Underworld arcade. The same sign was on the door. It was closed, too.

"Arggh!" Chip said in disgust. He wanted to rip down the sign and stamp on it. He jogged back to his house, grumbling all the way.

This was typical of the adults in Pine Hill, Chip thought. He had seen only one or two adults in The Meatball and The Underworld since they opened. He had never seen a town council member there. Yet somehow the adults were all experts. They thought that arcades were slimy pits full of bad language, smoking, alcohol, and drugs. And they thought the games were turning their kids into mindless, zonked-out game freaks.

Chip had never seen any evidence of drugs or alcohol at either the Meatball or The Underworld. Some of the kids occasionally tried to light up—either tobacco or pot—but they were usually caught and booted out the door. And nobody dared swear at the football players the arcades hired to maintain order. Not if they wanted to stay alive.

That evening, Chip and his dad went out to dinner. His dad let Sherwin come along, too. All Chip could think about were the two games arcades. Before he knew it, he was telling his dad about how they were being closed by the town council.

To Chip's surprise, Mr. Mitchell got very angry. "As soon as we finish dinner," he said, "we're going to that meeting."

Five minutes later, Chip stuffed a last bite of garlic bread into

67

his mouth. He and Sherwin followed Mr. Mitchell as he paid their bill and stalked out of the restaurant. As he rolled down the aisle between the tables, Sherwin waved good-bye. "My best wishes to *everybody*!" he said.

When they arrived, the council meeting was already in progress. The room was stuffed with kids, teachers, and parents. Chip recognized several kids from his school, including Kate Marconi.

Kate even got up and defended the games arcades. The kids in the audience cheered her. But the adults didn't look too impressed.

Then Chip had to listen to a bunch of boring adult speakers, and it made him want to spit. The adults got up and said the same things, over and over, about how kids were getting ruined by electronic games. The adults all called on the town council to close up the Meatball and The Underworld.

Then Mr. Fitzsimmons got up. Mr. Fitzsimmons was a big man. He had played football at Pine Hill High School. Now he was on the town council. He was really positive about computers, but he was opposed to video games. His daughter had gotten suspended from school for cutting classes to go to the Meatball and The Underworld. Mr. Fitzsimmons was on a personal crusade to close every arcade in Pine Hill.

"Don't get me wrong," he told the audience. "I think computers are great. I think all kids should have more exposure to computers—at home and in school. I think computers are the wave of the future. That's why I'm making a special presentation to the town council about a public government computer system, right after this hearing. I invite you all to attend. But computers are not video games."

The kids in the audience began booing and yelling. Sherwin was sitting on a chair beside Chip and his dad. Someone kicked the back of Sherwin's chair. The kick must have jarred Sherwin's circuits. He began running his JAIL GUARD program. He rotated his head and made his fire-siren sound. "Intruder alert!" he said. "Intruder alert!"

Everybody started laughing. Someone yelled, "Let the robot talk! Let the robot talk!"

Mr. Perkins, the mayor of Pine Hill, smacked his gavel on the table. "Order!" he said. "We must have complete silence, or you will be asked to leave this meeting."

Quickly, Chip reached over and pressed Sherwin's System Reset button. Pressing the button cleared Sherwin's memory. Once again, the little robot was silent. Then Chip got out the teaching pendant from his book bag and reloaded Sherwin's main program.

Mr. Fitzsimmons continued his speech. He claimed that although video games had computer microchips inside them, they were not computers because kids couldn't program them. Instead, the games programmed the kids. Mr. Fitzsimmons claimed that kids who played video games turned into glassy-eyed zombies. He said that kids who got hooked on video games became drug addicts, boozers, and crooks.

Chip's dad raised his hand and asked to speak. Video games, he said, had their bad points and were not good for children who already had emotional or psychological problems. But it was unfair of the adults in Pine Hill to close down the games arcades without even having visited one.

In addition, Chip's father said lots of psychologists and educators were in favor of games. Games arcades encouraged good grades by giving out free tokens for A's and B's on report cards. Arcade games were being set up in children's hospitals and in nursing homes. And the U.S. Army and the U.S. Air Force were setting up video games to train their soldiers. Some of the new racing-car games might even help young people become better, more alert drivers.

When Chip's dad finished talking, the kids went bonkers, applauding, stamping their feet, and cheering. Even some of the adults in the audience clapped. Now Chip was sure that the arcades would remain open.

But Mr. Fitzsimmons got up again.

"Mr. Mitchell is a smooth talker," he said. "He says that the arcades aren't causing any problems here in Pine Hill. But he's wrong. I have chilling evidence that the kind of sick, criminal thinking that video games promote is already infesting young people right here in Pine Hill.

"I have learned that last night at midnight, some young person got a computer to make dozens of calls to people in this community. Calls were made to all the members of the town council, the mayor, and others. And what kinds of calls did the computer make? Crank calls—dirty, sick crank calls.

"Who could have thought of such a devilish prank? Only a kid who knew about computers but had lost his sense of judgment because of his addiction to video games.

"I think that we should close up the arcades immediately before they spawn any new trouble in our community. This situation can only get worse. Today it's crank calls. Tomorrow it will be full-blown computer crimes like electronic bank robberies and snooping in other people's computers. We need to act now!"

When Mr. Fitzsimmons sat down, Mayor Perkins called for a vote on the issue. By a vote of 5 to 2, the town council decided to close down all the games arcades in Pine Hill.

The meeting was over. Chip and his dad got up to go. On their way out of the building, Mr. Fitzsimmons ran up to them and put his arm on Mr. Mitchell's shoulder. "No hard feelings, I hope," he said, smiling. "But I can't understand why you spoke in favor of video games, when your own sister, Libby, got one of those crank calls. You're not trying to protect anyone are you?" Mr. Fitzsimmons stared menacingly at Chip.

He suspects *me*! Chip thought in alarm. He thinks I programmed Hermes to make those crank calls.

Chip's dad looked at Chip. He noted how surprised his son was. He turned back toward Mr. Fitzsimmons. "I resent what you are implying," he said.

Mr. Mitchell stormed out the front door of the municipal building with Chip and Sherwin following. His dad wanted to head right home, but Chip had an idea. "You go on home," he said. "I think Sherwin and I'll go back in and listen to Mr. Fitzsimmons' sales pitch about his computers."

Chip and Sherwin returned to the meeting room and sat in the last row. Mr. Fitzsimmons wheeled a lot of expensive-looking computers into the room. Fifteen minutes later, his presentation began.

Mr. Fitzsimmons owned the largest business-computer store in Pine Hill. He was trying to convince council members to purchase his new portable business computers. The computers weighed only three pounds and fit in a small briefcase, yet they were as powerful as computers that were several times bigger.

Mr. Fitzsimmons' computers could be plugged into telephones and linked with the computers in the municipal building and with one another. The council members, many of whom lived far outside town, wouldn't even have to come to town to attend meetings. Instead, they could switch on their computers and attend the meetings electronically.

Mr. Fitzsimmons said that with the new two-way cable TV service in Pine Hill, town government could be computerized. The town's citizens could vote using their TVs. Town council members could ask people's opinions about controversial issues.

71

Mr. Fitzsimmons pushed a button on his computer. It began talking. First it talked in Mr. Fitzsimmons' voice, then in the voice of Mayor Perkins, and last in the voice of Margaret Atkins, the only woman member of the town council.

"You can use the telephone and leave one another mail in electronic mailboxes," Mr. Fitzsimmons said with a big grin. "And it wouldn't be mail made of words. It would be *voice* mail —in your voice or anyone else's."

Ms. Atkins raised her hand. "How private will these voice mail messages be?" she asked.

"Absolutely private," said Mr. Fitzsimmons. "If you get a phone call routed through the town computer, no one but you will know."

When Chip heard that, he stood up and ran to the front of the room. "Mr. Mayor," he said, "Mr. Fitzsimmons here thinks I made those crank calls last night. I didn't make them, but I know who did!"

WHO MADE THE MIDNIGHT CRANK CALLS?

(For the solution, turn to page 101.)

THE CASE OF
THE ZAPPED
OUTER — SPACE
GAME

It was a beautiful, sunny afternoon in late May. After track practice, Chip showered and changed. He made a quick trip to his homeroom locker.

He slammed the locker door shut and was preparing to leave when he heard someone spluttering and mumbling in his homeroom. He stuck his head inside the door to see who was in there.

It was Legs. "I wondered where you had disappeared to," Chip said, walking in the room. "You zipped off the track like a rocket."

"Darn this thing!" Legs said. He was bent over double beside a gray metal box that looked like a small air conditioner.

Legs' behind was stuck way up in the air. It was too tempting a target for Chip to resist. He swung his book bag like a baseball

73

bat and struck Legs square on the bottom. "Home run!" he cried.

"Hey!" said Legs. "Would you cut the clowning, please?"

He bent over again and fiddled with some wires behind the box.

"What is that thing?" Chip asked. "It looks like a bird feeder or something."

Legs had finally managed to unplug the box from the wall. He began winding up the electrical cord. "It's Frankie," he said.

"Hi, Frankie," Chip said, bowing to the box. "How d'you do?"

"He can't hear you," Legs said. "He's not turned on."

Legs picked up the box by a handle on its top. "Here," he said. "You can help me carry some of Frankie's books." He handed Chip a pile of textbooks and folders.

Chip looked at the books. "These books belong to that box?" he asked, puzzled.

"No, dopey," Legs said, grinning. The boys walked down the hall to the school office. Legs put the box on the counter.

He and Chip went out the front door of the school. "The books belong to Frankie del Burgo, over on Grandin Road—1416 to be exact. The box is an intercom. And it belongs to Frankie, too."

"So what are we doing with Frankie's books, and why were you carrying Frankie's intercom?" Chip asked.

"Frankie's a new guy," Legs said. "Just moved to Pine Hill. He's in our grade. His dad works for my dad."

"So?"

"So I'm going to carry his intercom and take him his books. He's handicapped. Auto crash. Both parents came out of it okay, but Frankie hurt his spine. I hear he can't use his arms or legs. He can't even climb out of bed. This intercom plugs into all of Frankie's classes. Frankie has one just like it in his bedroom. He can talk into his intercom, and we hear his voice in the class. And he can listen to his intercom and hear what's going on at school. Let's go meet him."

Twenty minutes later, Chip and Legs were walking up Grandin Road. "Frankie's must be the next house," Legs said, pointing.

As the boys passed the house right before Frankie's, they saw two men coming around the house from the backyard. The men were carrying a sack of peat moss to a station wagon parked in front of the house. They were dressed in business suits. "C'mon, Bert," the man in front said. "We don't have all day, y'know."

"Can it, Peters, wouldya?" the second man said. "If it wasn't for me, you'd still be twiddling bits at that bank in Raleigh."

Chip and Legs walked around the two quarreling men.

The boys rang the front doorbell at Frankie's. A teenaged boy answered the door.

Legs introduced himself and Chip. "This stuff's for Frankie," he said.

"I'm Greg, Frankie's older brother," the teenager said. "Come on in. I'll take you to Frankie's room." He led the boys back to Frankie's bedroom.

Chip and Legs were completely unprepared for what they saw. Frankie was lying in bed. Snakelike cables from machines around his room wound across the floor and climbed up the bed. Frankie was plugged in to all the machines. His body was the control center for the most dazzling set of electronics the boys had ever seen.

The bedroom looked like an electronics warehouse. Lining the walls were TVs, computers, robots, arcade games, and pinball machines. Mounted on the bedroom's far wall was a nine-foot TV screen. The screen was on. A soccer match was being televised. The noise from thousands of cheering people hit

75

the boys as they entered Frankie's room. The sound came from four coffee-table-sized speakers mounted in the corners of the room.

"Wow!" said Chip. "Where's the game coming from?"

"From Pakistan," said Greg.

"Pakistan?" asked Legs. His eyes opened wide.

"But how—" Chip asked.

"How do we get TV programs from Pakistan?" Greg said. "Simple. My mom and I built a satellite antenna to pick up extra programs for Frankie. Here, let me show you." He walked over to the window and pointed to the backyard.

Legs and Chip followed Greg to the window. In the backyard they saw a huge white bowl, tilted on its side and mounted on three metal legs.

"That's the antenna?" Legs asked.

"Right," said Greg. "It picks up a hundred and fifty TV programs from all across the world. The programs start in countries like Pakistan. They're bounced off a string of satellites that sit about twenty thousand miles up in the air, right over the equator. Within just a couple of seconds, they reach Pine Hill."

Chip stared at the antenna. It was as tall as a three-story building. Right behind the antenna, over in the next yard, he saw a square plot of ground covered with peat moss. Chip turned away from the window.

"Those signals take only a couple seconds," Legs was asking, "even when they come all the way from Pakistan?"

"Yep," said Gary. "Frankie can change the channels with just his voice. He says a new channel number, and instantly he 'jumps' thousands of miles to a different satellite and to a different part of the world. His electronic 'eyes' are as good as Superman's. In an instant Frankie can see things happening almost anywhere on the whole planet."

"What are those glasses you're wearing?" Legs asked Frankie. He leaned over and looked at Frankie's strange eyeglasses. The lenses looked as though they were made out of diamonds.

"Oh, these," Frankie laughed. "They're not real glasses. They're prisms. I can lie on my back, look straight up, and see the picture on the TV screen over there on the wall. The prisms bend the light so I don't have to sit up or prop up my head."

"And what's that next to your mouth?" Legs asked. He pointed to the black, rubbery object next to Frankie's mouth.

"That's a microphone," Frankie said. "I use it to control my computers and robots."

"Oh," Legs said. His brain was blinking a bright red "Tilt" light. "Where should I put these books?"

"Stand back," Frankie said. "Derrick," he said sharply, "come here."

Legs' mouth dropped open. A large table rolled across the room and stopped beside Frankie's bed. "Yes, master?" the table said.

"Down, Derrick . . . one-half meter," Frankie said.

"Yes, master," the table said. It lowered itself one-half meter.

"Okay, Legs," Frankie said. "Put the books on Derrick."

"What is this thing?" Legs said. He carefully put the books on Derrick the table.

"Derrick's a robot," Frankie said, grinning. "He just happens to be in the shape of a table. Almost all the things in my room are robots. My bed's a robot. My washstand's a robot. Watch this. I can—"

The phone rang. "Let me get it," Frankie said. "TV . . . sound off . . . phone . . . answer . . . hello, who's there?"

The sound from the soccer game stopped. A woman's voice came from all four speakers. "Hello?" it said. "Frankie? Greg?"

It was Greg and Frankie's mother. She was at her office and was calling about dinner. After a short conversation, she hung up.

"I better be checking my homework," Frankie said. Through his prism glasses, he winked at Greg.

"King . . . Kong . . . come . . . here," Frankie said. A robotic arm, mounted on a platform, rolled up to Frankie's bed. A control panel slipped out of the back of the arm and positioned itself only an inch from Frankie's head. Frankie rolled his head forward and stuck out his tongue and used it to push buttons on the control panel. Legs and Chip couldn't believe their eyes. Frankie was using his tongue to control King Kong the robotic arm.

By pushing different "arrow" buttons, Frankie made the arm open the homework on top of the books. He made the arm pick up a sheet of paper and tilt it toward him. It was his homework assignment from his adviser, Miss Phipps.

Frankie studied the paper. "Uh-huh," he said. "I'll be busy tonight." With a few quick flicks of his tongue, he had King Kong put the paper back and close the folder. "Corner . . . Kong," he commanded. The robotic arm rolled into the corner of the room behind the door.

A stoplight mounted on the wall beside the big TV screen started blinking green. Music from the movie *Star Wars* blared out of the speakers. "Oh, my gosh!" Frankie said. "Kal . . . time."

On the table near Frankie's closet, something that looked like a toaster oven said, "Five o'clock, master. Exactly."

Frankie got all excited. "Time for Dangerous Missions!" he said.

"What's that?" Chip asked.

"Frankie's favorite game," Greg said. "He plays it with a

friend outside of London, England. His friend is a quadriplegic, just like Frankie. They've been playing this game for more than a year. They've chased each other across the universe, time-warped into the future, and rescued whole galaxies. But the game still isn't over."

Chip and Legs sat down on the edge of Frankie's bed. Frankie's giant screen lit up with a sky blue display. On the display was a grid of crisscrossing white lines. "Those are the sectors in the Andromeda Galaxy," Greg whispered. "That's where Frankie and his friend Michael have been for the last month."

The game began. The screen changed with mind-dizzying speed. Sometimes it displayed a whole galaxy. Then Frankie would zoom in and display pictures of planetary systems within the galaxy. The next moment the screen would change again and show the vision you might see looking out the front window of a superfast space cruiser. Comets, suns, moons, and planets whizzed by as Frankie's spaceship hurtled across the An-dromeda Galaxy.

All of a sudden, there was a burst of static that was so loud it hurt the boys' ears. The screen exploded in a dazzling burst of red, orange, and green fireworks. Then it went blank.

"Must have been a direct hit on your ship from the enemy Zarkons," Greg said, turning to Frankie.

"No, Greg," Frankie said. "It wasn't that. The Zarkons were on the other side of the galaxy. It couldn't have been them. I think something's wrong with the equipment. Maybe a head crash on one of my disk drives."

Greg stared up at the empty screen. "That's the second time it's acted up today. First let me check the connections here in the room. Maybe something's loose."

Greg crawled around on the floor checking plugs, wires, and

cables. A moment later, a new display appeared on the video screen. Greg's head popped out from under Frankie's bed. "Did I get it?" he asked.

"I don't know what you got," Frankie said, looking through his prism glasses. "It isn't my game. It looks like some kind of data transmission." The screen looked like a giant sheet of white paper filled with symbols, numbers, and letters.

"Looks like pure cybercrud to me," Legs said.

"Maybe it's coded," suggested Chip. "Or else, like Legs says, maybe it's garbage from one of your satellites or computers."

"Code?" Frankie said. "Hmm. Kong . . . come . . . here." The robotic arm rolled up to the bed. "Greg," said Frankie, "get me the code directory for the local public-key codes. I got a hard copy from the computer just this morning. I think it's on Derrick under my homework."

"What are public-key codes?" Legs asked.

"I've heard about them," Chip said. "They're a way of turning computer messages into a secret code. Each person has two keys. One is secret, but the other one is open to the public. Anyone can see it."

"Right," said Frankie. He stuck out his tongue and made King Kong open the book of codes. "The public-key code most people use is called the Trapdoor Knapsack. It's based on an incredibly complicated mathematical formula.

"One of those lines of data up on the screen looks like a handshaking code that lets two computers talk to each other. It might point me to the public key that's published. Then we'd know where the stuff on the screen comes from."

"And why it's there instead of your game," said Greg.

With the help of King Kong, Frankie searched through his directory. "I think I have something," he said. "I'm going to run the screen through a decoding program on one of my computers."

Chip was amazed. "Your program can decode a message scrambled by the Trapdoor Knapsack?" he asked. "I read that it would take the fastest computer in the world a million years to do that."

Frankie grinned. "It's not my idea," he said. "It was in an article I read by an Israeli mathematician. I borrowed the idea from him.

"The trouble is, my program still hasn't been debugged, and it's full of kludges. But maybe it'll work."

Frankie gave a small, desktop computer beside his bed a few voice commands. A moment later, a message appeared at the top of its tiny screen. The computer also read the message out loud. "The . . . key . . . is . . . B+P4141," said the computer. "The title of the message is Los Angeles Central Bank—Electronic Funds Clearinghouse."

"Let's see what we've got here," Frankie said. "Computer . . . open file . . . slow scan."

The images on the screen disappeared. A moment later, the screen was filled with new numbers. The title of the screen was

```
*** FUNDS BEING TRANSFERRED ***
    (in Thousands of Dollars)
```

"Oh, my gosh!" Greg said. "This is really private information. We shouldn't be looking at this. It's probably against the law."

"Worse than that," Frankie said. "We shouldn't be getting it at all. The satellite antenna was pointed northeast toward England. Now it's pointed west toward Los Angeles."

Greg looked out the bedroom window. "You're right," he said. "But how'd it happen? To make the antenna point in a different direction, you'd need to have a wire connected to a computer. The only computer connected to the antenna's motor is the one in this room."

"Maybe it's not," Chip said, hopping off Frankie's bed. "Someone's tapping into your satellite computer system. And I know who."

WHO IS TAPPING INTO FRANKIE'S COMPUTERS?

(For the solution, turn to page 105.)

83

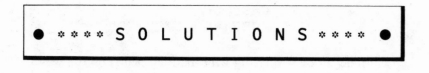

● �֍ �֍ ✖ SOLUTIONS ✖ ✖ ✖ ●

THE CASE OF
THE BURPING COMPUTER

Chip began by describing what had happened on the way to the Community Center. "Kate and her gang pretended that they were rescuing Hermes," he said. "But it was really an ambush.

"They fixed the Cart's rope so it would come loose on the steep hill. Then they waited in the woods near the bottom of the hill until the Cart and Hermes came rolling back down, out of control.

"They pretended to be on their way to the exterminators to debug their pillows, but it was all part of their ambush."

"That's a lie!" said Kate. "We went to the exterminators right after we left you."

Chip picked up a pillow with his free hand and threw it at Kate. "Then how come I can't smell any bug spray on your pillows?" he asked.

He continued. "The Panthers brought the pillows along so they could stop the Cart when it came back down the hill. Then they surrounded it so Legs and I couldn't see them messing with my computer."

"Messing? How?" Kate asked, her eyes flashing. "What do you think we were doing, feeding your computer to the fleas?"

"No!" said Chip, growing angry again. "You used a special machine I'd read about but never seen—until now. It has real thin wires that plug into the back of a circuit board, directly to a computer microchip.

"The machine works on electricity. It makes a copy of all the programs stored in microchip's read-only memory. Then it erases the memory. It's just like one of my ambush bugs. It attacks something by sucking out its insides."

"You've flipped!" Kate said. "Where would I get a machine like that?"

"Right here!" Chip said. He broke free from Miss Phipps' tight grip. Her fingernails had dug into his wrist. He ran to the back of the stage and grabbed the small maroon box he had seen earlier. Two fine wires danced above the box like antennas made out of silvery spider web.

Chip brought the box to the front of the stage. He thrust the box in Kate's face. "Why don't you tell Miss Phipps what's inside this box," he said.

"I won't!" Kate said. "Give it back! It's mine!"

Chip backed out of Kate's reach. "If you won't tell, then I will," he said. He unsnapped the top of the box and lifted it back on its hinges. Inside the box were lots of wires and microchips.

Chip turned toward Miss Phipps. "See this little chip in the center," he said. "It's a special kind of read-only memory. Kate's machine probably stored Hermes' music program on this chip. If you'll let me put the chip into Hermes, I bet he'll work just fine."

The kids in the audience began taking sides. A bunch of girls started chanting, "The Panthers win! The Panthers win!" Other kids, mostly boys, yelled, "Give Chip a chance!" The noise in the room was deafening.

"QUIET, *PLEASE!*" shouted Miss Phipps.

She looked at Kate. Then she looked at Chip. "All right, go ahead, Charles," she said, looking tired. "But if you're wrong, you're in big trouble."

Chip hopped off the stage and ran over to Legs. The boys wheeled Hermes back onto the stage. Chip opened his small tool case. He removed a memory chip from Hermes and replaced it with the chip from the maroon box. He put Hermes' top back on, plugged him in, and turned on his power.

Hermes' face came on the TV screen. His mouth opened wide. He began "singing" Beethoven's *Emperor* Concerto. Music from a piano, violins, cellos, flutes, clarinets, and other instruments poured from Hermes' speakers and rippled gloriously through the air. Legs put on his feathered troubadour hat and began flailing away at his air guitar. People cheered and whistled.

When Hermes and Legs were done playing, everyone—except the Panthers—stood on their chairs and clapped and stomped their feet.

Miss Phipps and the other judges held a hurried conference. Then Miss Phipps came back onto the stage. "The judges have decided," she said, "that the Panthers' computer was still the best in the contest—"

There were groans, shouts, and boos. The Panthers cheered.

Miss Phipps silenced the crowd with a fierce look. She continued. "But the Panther computer is disqualified for cheating. Therefore, the judges award the trophy to Chip, Legs, and Hermes."

THE CASE OF
THE MONKEY JAILBREAK

Chip was right! His house was being robbed. Thieves had parked a van in front of the house. When the police arrived, the thieves were putting Chip's computer, Hermes, into the van. They had already taken Aunt Libby's TV set and several of her prized statues.

The police rounded up the robbers, and only twenty minutes later, Hermes was back in Chip's bedroom, and the statues and TV were back in the living room.

Aunt Libby sat in the kitchen, trying to calm her nerves. She and Chip were sipping cups of hot cocoa.

"I still can't understand it, Charlie," she said. "How did you know that we were being robbed?"

Chip told Aunt Libby about Sherwin's "bat squeaks" and about the robot's encounter in Chip's bedroom with Mandrake the monkey. "Sherwin is programmed to ignore kids and small adults, like you, Aunt Libby," he said. "But he thinks anything else that moves is a monkey. When we saw Sherwin going crazy at the back door, I knew he must have spotted something."

"But how did you know it wasn't Mandrake?" Aunt Libby asked.

"That was easy," Chip said. "I latched my bedroom door from the outside before I came down to help you. Even Mandrake's not smart enough to unlock a door that's locked on the other side."

THE CASE OF
THE HAUNTED HOTEL

Mr. Janoweitz, Chip, Legs, and half a dozen other kids trooped down the dark fire escape stairs to the fifth floor of the hotel. Using Mr. Janoweitz's flashlight they found room 544.

At the door to the room, they met up with the manager of the hotel and four hotel security guards whom Mr. Janoweitz had called. Then, at the count of three, the guards burst into the room.

The lights in the room were on. The room was filled with people. In the center of the room, sitting on a queen-sized bed pulled out from the wall, was the huge, hulking wizard Chip and Legs had seen in the lobby. His little robot familiars danced around him, on top of the bed. In his lap was a computer keyboard.

A guard rushed toward the surprised wizard and grabbed the keyboard. The others formed a ring around the TV set mounted on the left wall. Everybody looked up. On the screen was a list of the major hotel computer functions:

```
      *** HOTEL MARQUIS ***
   MASTER COMPUTER CONTROL

      1. electronic mail
      2. calculator
      3. video games
      4. room computers
      5. laundry
      6. snack shop
      7. restaurant
      8. room service
      9. electronic shopping
     10. hotel alarm system

   Type a number (1-10) to select a
   function:
```

The manager turned to the wizard and said, "I am placing you and your friends under the custody of my guards. The police are on their way. You will be turned over to them as soon as they arrive."

An hour later, Chip and Legs were seated in the hotel manager's office. The lights in the hotel were back on. Upstairs in the kids' room on the fourteenth floor, everything was back to normal.

"But how did you guess that this wizard fellow was responsible for the hotel computers' problems?" the manager asked.

"I realized that something like this was possible," Chip said, "after the hotel fire alarm went off. When we came back to our room, I studied the information in the room about the hotel computers. It showed how the room computers were connected to the lights, TV, smoke detector, telephones, and fire alarm. And all the room computers were linked to the hotel's main minicomputer.

"But I made the real connection when the TV started going crazy," said Chip. "It flashed a picture of Saturn on the screen, and that reminded me of the painting of Saturn on the wizard's hat.

"Then I asked my watch the time. It said 'Nine thirty.' The wizard's sign had said that the demonstration of his powers would begin at eight o'clock. That was when the hotel fire alarm went off. After eight o'clock, the hotel went crazy. The 'haunting' started then.

"I called the front desk, and the hotel clerk told me that the room where the fire alarm went off was 544. 544 was the wizard's room. That convinced me. Then I was sure that he was behind everything."

"But the wizard was outside while the fire fighters inspected the hotel," said Legs. "I know, because I saw him."

"I saw him, too," said Chip. "He knew there was no fire, but he ran out of the hotel so nobody would get suspicious."

"How did you know that he was capable of taking over the entire hotel through the room computers?" asked Mr. Janoweitz.

"I didn't know he could," Chip said. "But I did know that he must be a computer expert. Those little robot creatures of his are far more advanced than the robots you can buy in stores. Any person who is that good with robots must also be good with computers."

THE CASE OF
THE RUNAWAY ROLLER COASTER

"Do you use arrays to control the volcano car's speed?" Chip asked the men.

"We do!" said the man at the computer terminal. "How did you—"

"Never mind," Chip said. "If you can, try to change the loops around. Put the inside loop on the outside, and put the outside loop on the inside. That might be your problem."

The man who was standing up looked at Chip. "Who are you, anyway?" he asked. "How could you know—"

"Wait, George," the other man said. "I think the kid's got something. Let me try it. It's our last hope."

The man's fingers flew over the computer keyboard. Computer commands flashed on the display screen and disappeared. The man looked up at Chip. "These are the two loops," he said, pointing at the screen.

Chip leaned over and peered at the screen. This is what he saw:

```
FOR SPEED = 1 TO 8
  FOR CIRCLE = 1 TO 8
    LET CAR = CHART (SPEED, CIRCLE)
    GOSUB 5000 'ADJUST SPEED OF CAR MOTOR
  NEXT CIRCLE
NEXT SPEED
```

"Okay," Chip said. "Switch them!"

The man pressed some buttons. The inside loop became the outside loop, and the outside loop became the inside loop:

```
FOR CIRCLE = 1 TO 8
  FOR SPEED = 1 TO 8
    LET CAR = CHART (SPEED, CIRCLE)
    GOSUB 5000 'ADJUST SPEED OF CAR MOTOR
  NEXT SPEED
NEXT CIRCLE
```

When the man was done making the changes, Chip asked, "Can you patch this change into the program that's running now?"

"I think so," the man said nervously. Trickles of sweat ran down his cheeks and dripped on his shirt collar. "There. I did it. Now we can only watch and see what happens."

Everybody looked up at the big video monitor.

The volcano car with the sixteen people on board was still climbing up the inside wall of the volcano. It was still going fast.

Then it started to slow down. Slower. Slower.

It reached the top of the volcano. It stopped.

It hesitated just a moment, then, as it was supposed to, it followed the transparent track down into the center of the volcano and out the hole in the bottom. A moment later, the video screens showed the car pulling up and stopping at the station outside the volcano. Everybody in the underground computer control room cheered.

After things calmed down, the two men asked Chip how he had known about the problem with the loops and the arrays in their program. He explained that he hadn't known whether or not his solution would work. It had been a desperate but lucky guess.

Chip had gotten the idea when he heard the programmer mention that the computer seemed to be feeding the wrong speeds to the car's motor. He had said the order in which the numbers were sent seemed upside-down or backward.

This reminded Chip of the conversation he and Legs had had with the technician at the Space Shuttle Simulator about numbers that were upside-down and backward.

"But why did this happen?" Chip asked. "How did the loops get reversed? They worked earlier in the day."

One of the men explained that during the lunch break when the volcano ride was shut down, he and the other man had been testing new programs on the control computer. The program that had been in operation when Chip and Legs rode the cars through the volcano had had some minor bugs, so the men had replaced it with a backup program.

"We use an array to store the car's different speeds as it climbs the inside wall of the volcano," said the man. "The car makes eight complete circles around the volcano, so we have eight different columns in the array. And the car's speed has to be adjusted eight times while it is whizzing around each circle. So we have eight different rows in the array."

The man punched a few buttons on his terminal. "Here's what the array looks like. The up-and-down columns of numbers represent the eight different circles. Each sideways row represents one of the car's eight speeds within a circle."

The man continued explaining: "The inside loop was supposed to read each of the eight speeds for each circle. Those speeds are in the rows. After eight speed adjustments, the car would have gone onto a new circle. And the outside loop would have switched the computer to a new column. The column would have had eight new speeds. The inside loop would have read them and sent them to the car.

"But by accident, the two loops were reversed. That's why the speeds were haywire. The outside loop thought the eight

25	24	27	28	22	24	24	26
26	23	27	29	21	25	22	23
24	25	25	30	22	23	21	25
22	25	21	31	24	26	22	24
23	26	23	30	25	27	24	27
25	26	24	29	25	26	26	29
28	29	28	31	28	29	30	32
31	32	33	35	32	34	35	36

rows represented the eight circles. The inside loop thought each column was one of the speeds within a single circle. This made the computer read the speeds across the columns rather than from the top of each column down to the bottom. The speeds in the top row were read first, the speeds in the next row second, and so on. The last speeds were the high speeds in the bottom row. When they were sent to the car, it went faster and faster. Without an adjustment, the car would have crashed."

The park officials praised Chip for his quick thinking. To show their appreciation, they gave Chip and Legs a free one-day pass to all the rides at Fantasy World.

THE CASE OF
THE ROBOT WARRIORS

When Sleepy saw the robot trainer point to the yellow shed, he remembered spotting Karhonda coming from that same shed earlier in the morning.

The shed had been dark, but Karhonda had admitted that there were robots inside. She had said that the robots were fat women.

Before Sleepy could see anything else, Karhonda had dragged him away to the Outer-Space Pavilion. Now Sleepy was sure that the two robots in the shed had been Rachet and Bertha.

But what had Karhonda been doing in the shed?

Sleepy guessed that she had gone in there to turn on Rachet's infrared switch because she was plotting with Kate to beat Chip in the Robot Warriors game.

"But how did Kate get Bertha and Chip get Rachet?" Sleepy asked.

Chip explained to Sleepy that when the Robot Warriors arena opened, Kate made sure she and Chip were the first in line. Then, before the trainer could assign the robots to her and Chip, Kate had asked for Bertha. That way she made sure that Chip got Rachet.

"Now I see," said Sleepy. "For Kate and Karhonda's plan to work, Kate had to make sure that you two were the first people to operate the robots. Otherwise the trainer would have discovered that the infrared switch was on before you had begun your battle."

"So that's why Kate woke me up before dawn and hustled me down to the robots' arena," said Chip. "It was all part of her plot."

"There's still something I don't understand," said Sleepy. "If Rachet's infrared sensor was already turned on, why didn't she chase after the trainer when he turned on her power, in the yellow shed?"

The boys asked the trainer. This is how he explained it:

When he brought the robots to the arena, Rachet didn't

notice his body heat because she was not in Fight mode. Instead, she was in Transport mode, so that the trainer could move her and Bertha to the arena from the yellow shed. While in Transport mode, Rachet's microchip brains were programmed to ignore the signal from the infrared sensor.

When the match began, Chip pressed the red Fight button. This shifted the robot into Fight mode. Now Rachet's microchip brain paid attention to the signals from the infrared sensor. When Rachet was running away from Kate's robot, she got close enough to Chip to sense his body heat, and she headed right toward him. This explains why she crashed into Chip's platform. Rachet had sensed Chip's body heat and was trying to "find" him.

When the trainer finished his explanation, Sleepy and Chip angrily accused the girls of having rigged the battle between the robot warriors.

At first Kate and Karhonda denied everything. But the robot trainer recalled having seen Karhonda the day before, battling robots in the arena and hanging around when he closed up the arena and walked the robots back to the shed.

"You can't get away with this!" Chip said. "You tried to kill me!"

"No we didn't," Kate said. "Maybe we did set you up. But we didn't count on Rachet being so strong. We expected her to hug the platform and stop. Then we were going to have Bertha come to the rescue. That way our robot, Bertha, was a sure winner."

"So you admit everything," said Sleepy.

The girls nodded. They confessed that they had cooked up the idea for the rigged contest more than a month earlier when Kate, like Chip, had seen the robot warriors article in the science magazine. From the article she had learned about the purpose and location of the robots' infrared sensors. After Chip had foiled her plan at the computer music contest, she wanted revenge.

Karhonda had spent the previous day learning how to operate the robots' control boxes so she could coach Kate.

After the robots were returned to the shed, the robot trainer accompanied the young people back to their room at the Marquis Hotel and spoke to Mr. Janoweitz, the lead teacher for the class trip.

Mr. Janoweitz sat with the girls on the long bus ride back to Pine Hill. "I won't tell your parents about this," he said. "But I'm not going to let you off the hook either. You two think you're so sharp at programming robots, I've got the perfect job for you."

Kate and Karhonda exchanged nervous glances. "What job, Mr. Janoweitz?" Kate asked.

"We've got a new crew of janitorial robots," said Mr. Janoweitz, smiling. "I want you to program them to take out the trash."

"Yuck," said Karhonda.

"When do we start programming them?" Kate asked.

"Right now," said Mr. Janoweitz. He pulled two *Robot Programmers' Manual*s the size of dictionaries out of his briefcase and dropped them on the girls' laps. "I was studying these on the trip," he said, "so I could do the programming myself. But why should I program robots when I've got two experts?

"You better get busy," he said. "The first trash collection is tomorrow morning. If the robots don't pick up the trash, I'll need two humans instead. I bet you can guess who I'll pick."

THE CASE OF
THE COMPUTER SCAPEGOAT

"Cheating!" Mr. Randolph cried. "What are you talking about? Wren, let go of these two. I want to hear what they have to say."

Reluctantly, the other man let go of Chip and Legs. "I don't think this is wise," he said.

"I'll decide what's wise," said Mr. Randolph. He looked at Chip. "Well?" he said.

Chip explained to Mr. Randolph how he and Legs had discovered Radley Moser. He explained that Radley seemed to be starving for lack of money.

Chip pulled out Radley's form from the Social Security office. He gave it to Mr. Randolph. "Mr. Moser says your computer is broken," Chip said. "Is that true? Does it swallow people's records?"

Mr. Randolph took the form and studied it. "No," he said. "Our computer works fine. Why?"

Chip explained that both Radley and Mr. Wren had said that Radley didn't get his money because the computer had swallowed it.

"That's nonsense!" Mr. Randolph said.

"Nonsense?" Chip said. "Look at this." He pointed at the place on the form where it listed Radley's account number. "It says MKW 30449."

"So?" said Mr. Randolph.

"So that's the same number that's on Mr. Wren's name badge. And the initials MKW can't stand for Radley Moser. But they could stand for Myron K. Wren."

Mr. Randolph looked at the form. Then he looked at his employee's name badge. "All right, Wren, what's going on here?" he asked.

Wren shrugged his shoulders. "Beats me," he said. "I think the kid is just trying to make trouble."

"We'll see about that," said Mr. Randolph. He got on the intercom and called in the head of the department. After being questioned for about fifteen minutes, Wren admitted that Radley Moser had not gotten his Social Security check for two months in a row.

At that point, Mr. Randolph told the boys that they'd better leave. He promised to get back in touch with them as soon as possible. Chip and Legs gave Mr. Randolph their phone numbers and quickly left.

The next day Chip got a phone call. It was Mr. Randolph. In trying to help one old man, Mr. Randolph said, the boys had uncovered something far bigger and more serious.

Apparently, the winter before, a number of the Social Security office clerks had formed a conspiracy with a social service department programmer. They had processed the computer records to look as if Social Security recipients were getting their monthly checks. Instead, the checks, or portions of them, were being siphoned off into the programmer's and the clerks' own accounts.

The conspirators made sure that all the accounts they tampered with belonged to people who were either very old or very feeble. That way, the people couldn't defend themselves. Like Radley Moser, when they didn't get their money, they may have complained. But Wren and the other clerks told them that it was the computer's fault. The computer, they said, had swallowed the people's checks. After a while, the people despaired.

Luckily, Chip and Legs had found Radley just in time. And in helping Radley, they had uncovered a case of criminal fraud in the Social Security office. Mr. Randolph promised Chip that

100

the criminals who had defrauded Radley and the other people would be rounded up immediately and put on trial.

THE CASE OF
THE MIDNIGHT CRANK CALLS

When Mr. Fitzsimmons spoke to Chip and his dad after the hearing on the arcade games, something he said sounded suspicious. Chip listened to Mr. Fitzsimmons' computer sales pitch again, hoping it would help him remember what had been said.

Chip heard Mr. Fitzsimmons say that the town's computer voice mail would be absolutely private.

Yet Mr. Fitzsimmons had known about Aunt Libby's crank call. Who had told him? Not Chip. Not his dad. And certainly not Aunt Libby.

He had known, Chip figured, because Mr. Fitzsimmons had programmed a computer to make the call. Just as he had programmed a computer to make all the other crank calls—precisely at midnight.

But according to Aunt Libby, the caller wasn't a computer, it was a kid. When Chip heard Mr. Fitzsimmons' computer talking in different voices, he realized that Mr. Fitzsimmons could program his computer to have any voice he wanted. It was a snap for him to create a kid's voice. He could create two messages—one for men, another for women—then have the computer dial numbers all around town and replay the messages, over and over, on the telephone.

Chip accused Mr. Fitzsimmons of making the phone calls and of using his computer to make it seem as though the crank caller was a kid.

Mr. Fitzsimmons had made the calls for two reasons, Chip

said. First, Mr. Fitzsimmons wanted to convince the council that arcade games were bad, and that they turned kids into criminals.

Second, Mr. Fitzsimmons wanted to scare the council into thinking that video-game-trained kids would soon be tapping their phone lines and stealing their computer files. Then the council would be willing to buy his computers—the ones that could make "absolutely private" phone calls and protect the town's electronic information.

When Chip finished talking, Mr. Fitzsimmons denied everything. To Chip's disappointment, Mayor Perkins and the town council were inclined to agree with Mr. Fitzsimmons. They thought Chip's story sounded too farfetched to be true.

Chip had failed. Unless . . .

He ran behind Mr. Fitzsimmons' computer and dumped Mr. Fitzsimmons' package of disks on the table.

Sherwin came rolling up to the front of the meeting room. When Chip had jumped up from his seat, he had accidentally bumped the robot and depressed the "1" key on Sherwin's head. Pressing the "1" key automatically put Sherwin into his sentry program. Sherwin assumed he was in Chip's bedroom. His primary job was to be on guard for a prison break by Mandrake the monkey. To Sherwin, a "monkey" was anyone smaller—or bigger—than a kid.

When Sherwin reached the front of the room, the nearest adult was Mr. Fitzsimmons. He spotted Mr. Fitzsimmons on his ultrasonic sensor. Sherwin's red LED eyes started flashing. He made his police-siren whistle. He rolled up to Mr. Fitzsimmons, raised his pincer hand, and grabbed Mr. Fitzsimmons on the knee. "Bad monkey!" Sherwin said. "Get back in your cage!"

Mr. Fitzsimmons howled. "Get this creature off me!" he

cried. He tried to pull away from Sherwin, but Sherwin held him tight. "Naughty, naughty monkey," Sherwin said.

Sherwin's arrival gave Chip a few valuable moments to search through the disks. Desperately, he picked out a disk marked Arcade. He popped the disk into Mr. Fitzsimmons' computer.

The disk booted up a program automatically. "Hello, cutie," the computer said. "I've been watching you. D'you want to go out on a date sometime?"

"Hey!" said Margaret Atkins. "That's the voice of the kid who called me last night. That's the crank caller!"

The computer continued talking. "Want to hear a dirty joke?" it asked.

"We do not!" Mayor Perkins said. He marched up to the computer and yanked out its plug.

Chip ran over to Sherwin. "No monkey," he said. "Big person." Sherwin released Mr. Fitzsimmons' knee and rolled away.

Mayor Perkins turned to Chip. "Young man," he asked, "is that your robot?"

"Yes, sir," Chip said.

"Do you also program computers?" the mayor asked.

"Yep," said Chip.

"And do you play video games?" asked the mayor.

"Oh, yeah," said Chip. "Especially the new videodisc games!"

The mayor smiled. Then he turned toward the members of the council. "I believe we owe this young man and all the other young people of this community an apology. If this young man is an example of what video games do to young people, then I'm in favor of video games."

Mr. Fitzsimmons began protesting. "I think you're making a big—"

"Quiet, Fitzsimmons!" said the mayor. "I no longer care what you think. I'm suspending you from the council, pending an investigation into this whole affair.

"I don't know about you other members of the council who voted to close down the game arcades," said the mayor. "But I make a motion that we hold another vote right now."

The council voted again, this time without Mr. Fitzsimmons. Mayor Perkins and Margaret Atkins changed their votes. Their switch made the difference. By a vote of 4 to 2, the arcades would stay open.

THE CASE OF
THE ZAPPED OUTER-SPACE GAME

"Legs," Chip said, "what were the names of those two guys next door who were carrying that bag of peat moss?"

"Bert and . . . Peters, I think," Legs said.

"Right," said Chip. "And what's the address of the house next door?"

"Well," said Legs, "the address is probably two numbers lower than this house's number. This house is, um—"

"1416 Grandin Road," Frankie said.

"Right," said Legs. "So their house must be 1414 Grandin. But who cares?"

"I care," Chip said. "These facts are clues. And if we put the clues together, they mean something. First you take the number 1414 and turn it around. Then what do you have?"

"4141," said Legs after a moment. "But—"

"Then," said Chip, "if you take the first letter in Bert's name and the first letter in Peters' name and add to them the backwards street number of their house, what do you get?"

"BP4141," Greg said.

"Correct," said Chip. "Does that remind you of anything?"

"It sure does!" Frankie said excitedly. "It's almost the same as B+P4141. And that's the public-code key used by the people who zapped my game and somehow took control of our antenna."

"You think it's Bert and Peters?" Legs asked.

"I do," said Chip. "Those guys looked suspicious the moment we saw them."

"You mean carrying the peat moss to their car?"

"Yes," said Chip. "They were carrying peat moss, and they looked like they had been gardening. But they didn't act like gardeners."

"And they were wearing business suits," said Legs.

"Right," said Chip.

"Is that it?" Greg asked.

"No," said Chip. "Take a look out the back window."

Legs and Greg looked out the back window again. "What do you see?" asked Frankie.

Greg turned around. He smiled. "Frankie," he said, "there's a garden behind Bert and Peters' house. It's covered with peat moss. And it's right next to our antenna."

Frankie grinned. "It's not a garden at all, is it?" he said. "It's an underground wire that's tapping into our antenna. The garden is just a cover."

"Exactly," said Chip. "The other end of that wire probably leads to a computer inside Bert and Peters' house. And Bert and Peters are probably using that computer right this minute to siphon thousands of dollars out of the money being piped around the country electronically by that Los Angeles bank."

"Wow!" said Frankie. "This is a real dangerous mission right in my own bedroom. Maybe if we get the police over here real quick, we'll be able to catch those two crooks."

"First," said Chip, "let's call my dad. He'll help us get through to the police. If we went to the police on our own with a story like this, they'd think the whole thing was a joke."

Frankie used voice-entry commands to dial Chip's father. He and Chip explained the situation to Mr. Mitchell.

Ten minutes later, Mr. Mitchell and two squad cars pulled up in front of Bert and Peters' house. The police had a search warrant. They found the two men still at a computer terminal in the living room.

Chip had been right. The terminal was wired to Frankie's satellite antenna. The men were illegally tapping the Los Angeles bank's transmission of "electronic money" to banks in New York.

The men were using Frankie's antenna because they believed that if their activities were discovered, Frankie and Greg would be blamed. It was their antenna, and they were well known computer whiz kids. While the police were investigating them, Bert and Peters could slip away unnoticed.

The two men had been siphoning off only four-tenths of a cent on each dollar transmitted. The money they siphoned off went temporarily to private accounts in Raleigh, North Carolina, under dummy names. Then the men planned to transmit it overseas to a secret account in Zurich, Switzerland. In Switzerland, the money would have been beyond the reach of U.S. authorities.

But wouldn't the bank in New York discover the missing money? Banks balance their books exactly—even down to $\frac{1}{10}$ of a cent.

Bert and Peters had covered all their tracks. They were very smart programmers. And Peters had worked in a big Raleigh bank for several years. To hide their theft, they had created a clever program to "round off" the amount of money actually sent to a bank receiving a "shipment" of electronic money.

When they did this, the stolen ⁴/₁₀ of a cent simply disappeared. The bank in New York never knew it existed.

After a theft, a dollar arrived in New York worth only 99 and ⁶/₁₀ cents. The bank computer in New York would have noticed this. But before it had a chance to check it, the program rounded the 99 and ⁶/₁₀ cents back to 100 cents—a full dollar! The stolen ⁴/₁₀ of a cent had vanished without a trace!

How could the thieves get a New York bank's computer to use their program? Simple. When the bank received the shipment of electronic money in the form of a data transmission, the thieves' program was tacked on the end, masquerading as data. Once the program penetrated the bank computer's security, it ordered the computer to obey it immediately. The computer ran the crooked program, and a fraction of each incoming dollar disappeared.

But why would Bert and Peters go to all this trouble to rob ⁴/₁₀ of a cent?

Four-tenths of a cent per dollar sounds like a small amount. But the Los Angeles bank transmitted a hundred million dollars a week. That meant Bert and Peters would be siphoning four hundred thousand dollars a week into their private accounts.

The next day at school, Legs carried Frankie's "talk box" around to all of Frankie's classes. Each time he plugged his friend in, the two boys exchanged jokes and talked about their adventure the day before.

Legs bragged about The Case of the Zapped Outer-Space Game to all the kids. Everybody was very impressed. Especially the girls.

Chip ran into Legs in the hallway on the way to an afternoon class. He tapped the intercom with his finger. "Well, Detective Legs," he said, "you and Frankie and I are getting the reputation of being high-tech crime fighters. When do we tackle our next case?"

"No more cases," said Legs. "This time it's space adventure. I'm going over to Frankie's house this afternoon. He's making me his copilot in the Dangerous Missions game. Right after we watch a track meet in Tanzania, we're blasting off to explore the universe's biggest black hole!"

KATE AND CHIP'S
OFFICIAL
HACKER'S DICTIONARY

Array A way of storing information in a computer. An array looks like a piece of graph paper with lots of little boxes. Each box is a cubbyhole in the computer's memory where you can put some information.

Bit A computer 1 or 0.

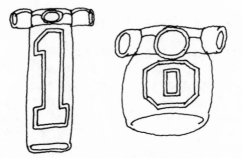

Bletch Disgusting!

Bug (1) A mistake in your program. (2) A little microchip. With all its tiny legs, it looks like a caterpillar or a beetle!

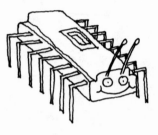

Byte Eight bits, all lined up in a row. (Like tall kids and short kids in the cafeteria line, the tall kids are 1's, the short kids are 0's.)

Crock A mixed-up program. Needs to be cleaned up.

Crufty Too complicated. KISS (Keep It Simple, Stupid!).

Cuspy Very, very good.

Cybercrud (1) Mixed-up, meaningless, or useless information. (See <u>Garbage Collection.</u>) (2) When people use big computer words to fool you into thinking they're smart.

112

Debugger A hacker who's good at tracking down tricky bugs.

Decode A decoding program translates information in a secret code into English.

Dink When you make one tiny change and it destroys your whole program.

FOR-NEXT A pair of commands in BASIC. They put the computer into a loop. It goes around in a circle and obeys the same commands over and over. The first command in the loop is FOR. The last is NEXT. The loop can be empty or have lots of other commands.

Frob Twiddle, fool with.

Garbage Collection Getting rid of garbage (stray commands or data) in the computer's memory.

Glitch Electronic noise. Makes the computer go bananas.

Glork! Wow! Oh, no!

GOTO A command in BASIC. It tells the computer to jump

from one line to another in
your program. Too many GOTO
commands make the computer hop
around like a dizzy kangaroo.

Gronk Out Go home and crash
(sleep).

Gweep A hacker who is real
tired. (Gweeps should all
gronk out, or they're liable
to make dinks and mung their
computer.)

Hackers Us (Kate and Chip)!
People who know computers
inside out. Supersharp
programmers. (<u>Not</u> a dumb
"user." See <u>User</u>.)

Hairy In the clouds, rare,
expert. (When you see a
20-foot-long program, you say:
"Hey! That's a hairy
program!")

Handshaking When two computers
talk to each other. "Did you
get all that data?" one
computer asks. "Yeah!" says
the other computer.

Hard Copy When a computer types
a message, a program, or a
picture on a piece of paper.

Head Crash When the read / write head on your disk drive divebombs the disk and digs a hole in it. Bye, bye, floppy!

Kludge (Rhymes with <u>stooge</u>.) When somebody tries to patch up a buggy program with glue, tape, and rubber bands—a real mess!

LED Light Emitting Diode. Many LEDs are grouped together to create calculator displays and robotic eyes.

Loop When a computer goes around in a circle, obeying the same commands over and over. If you want to make your computer dizzy, try this loop: 10 GOTO 10. It's an infinite loop. The computer can't escape.

Memory Dump When you print out everything in a computer's memory. (Like to see if anybody is messing around with your computer.)

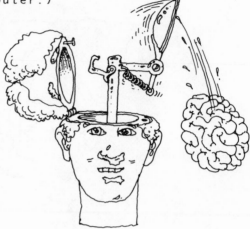

Munch Two bytes.

Mung Chewing or chopping up a program. When you are in a panic, you mung a program. (You destroy it, but you don't mean to.)

Nerd A hacker gone bad.

116

Nybble Half a byte.

Phrog A real gross person—half turkey and half toad.

Pixel Picture element. A point or box on a computer's video screen. The computer can fill in the pixel with a color. All the colored pixels, together, make up a picture.

POM Phase of the Moon. Flaky! A hacker who stays up all night programming and eating pepperoni pizza gets real POM.

Sensors Microchips on a robot's body. Sensors are the robot's "senses." An <u>infrared</u> sensor is like a thermometer—it lets the robot sense heat. <u>Ultrasonic</u> sensors are like bat "radar." They bounce sound waves off objects. The way the waves return tells the robot the objects' shape and where the objects are located. <u>Tactile</u> sensors give the robot a sense of touch. <u>Voice recognition</u> gives the robot "ears."

Spazz A hacker who is out of control.

Teaching Pendant A control box used to program a robot or operate the robot by remote control.

Tree A way of storing information in a computer. Each little piece of information sits on a tree branch or a twig.

User A person who uses computers but doesn't understand them. A real loser—a "luser."

Wizard An expert. A superhacker.

Worm A string of 8 bits (a byte).

KATE'S COMPUTER WORMS

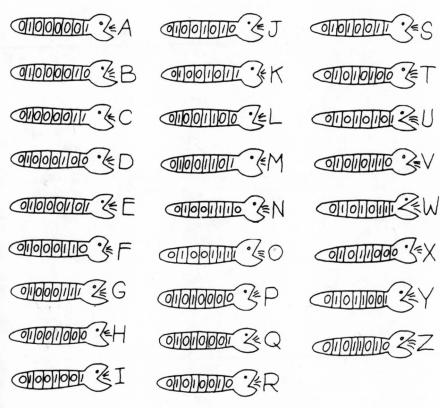